CONCIERGE ANTHOLOGY

A NEW ADVENTURE

A Collection Of Work From Those Who Make
The Writers' Rooms Possible

Erin Casey and Alex Penland, ed.

For our concierges, our community, and every rising star.

Table Of Contents

Introduction

Dear Reader, thank you for your support of The Writers' Rooms! By picking up this book, you have made your first step into joining our community as a whole.

TWR is an organization which endeavors to create a safe, inclusive community for all writers. We believe that everyone has a wealth of knowledge and a story to share. In our Rooms (which are community-led, genre-based gatherings), you bring both to the table. Each meeting consists of both discussions and time to write. Our events, which are held in conjunction with local businesses and libraries, offer a safe space in which to meet other members of your local writing community.

Our Rooms are led by volunteer Concierges. This book is our thanks to them. Inside is a compilation of their work revolving around one theme: "Beginnings". As each Concierge leads a genre-specific Room, you will find this theme displayed across a broad spectrum of literature. These pages include works of poetry, flash fiction, horror-noir, fantasy, and romance. We love and appreciate our Concierges, and we are so delighted to share their work with the community.

To our Concierges: thank you. We could not do this without you.

We hope you enjoy the 2018 Concierge Anthology from The Writers' Rooms! There will be more to come.

Best,
Erin Casey and Alex Penland, TWR Directors

Casey

Casey (no relation to Erin Casey) is a twenty-something human who stares at blank word-processor screens and calls it writing. They're a Concierge of the Rainbow Room, they work with adult students on developing life and work skills, and they're a professional jack-of-all-trades for hire (petsitting, babysitting, housesitting, tech support). They also hold the dubious honor of Vogon Poetry Champion of ICON in Cedar Rapids, two years running.

Casey likes to read stories with really good character development (or really bad puns) in book or webcomic form, listen to an unexpectedly broad range of music, and get excited about nerdy things. They also like animals of most varieties and useless trivia.

They are on Twitter @copingmechanism.

The Writer Wakes

Casey

In the morning the writer is empty
And with first waking breath inhales words.
Like scaffolding, like frame-words, familiar,
The first words: I Am.
tired rested warm cold
short tall slim fat gay straight
Not enough just enough loved alone
I Have To.
pee grab breakfast get some water shower
pay that bill call someone get to work
wake up
I Want To.
write
And with that the floodgates the clamor
The city inside begins to stir
And a hundred thousand lives speak their stories
And the writer rushes to take note
Their day begun.

Eliza David

Eliza David is the erotic romance author of eleven self-published novels, including the Cougarette series. She was born and raised on the noisy South Side of Chicago, but now lives in quiet Iowa City, one of the renowned Cities of Literature. A member of the Romance Writers of America (RWA), Eliza also maintains a local literary presence, serving on the Iowa City Public Library's Board of Trustees, moderating the romance writing group at the Iowa Writers' House, and serving as an annual headlining author at the Iowa City Book Festival. In addition to writing the naughty words, Eliza is a blogger as well, having served as a contributing writer for Real Moms of Eastern Iowa, The Good Men Project, and Thirty on Tap. She was most recently featured in Best Women's Erotica, Volume 4. Her next project, The Lamar St. Jon Experience, is currently out for query.

You can follow Eliza on Facebook (ElizaDWrites), Twitter(@elizadwrites), Instagram(writegirlproblems), or on her blog at www.elizadavidwrites.com.

Unisex

Eliza David

"Frankie? Is that you?"

She recognized the voice of her ex-husband but didn't want to believe her ears. Frankie turned at the hand dryer to see Jeff, waving at her. He seemed happy. Too happy to be fresh off of a divorce, no matter how amicable it seemed. She gave an awkward smile back as silent acknowledgment. It was her first time seeing him since their divorce was finalized three months before but it felt like she was seeing him for the first time in her life.

Jen, her best friend since they started at St. Agnes twenty years ago, asked her how she could leave a man like Jeff. Franks, he's perfect, she'd purr. Great job, good body, still has all of his hair. She went on, listing Jeff's physical attributes (which were quite exquisite, Frankie even had to admit) as if his ability to inherit top notch genes was were enough to make her stay in the world's most boring marriage.

And here he was, being the opposite of boring in a unisex bathroom of a nightclub both of them were too old to be in.

"Jeff," she started, moving out of the way of a gentleman easing his sopping wet hands into the high tech hand dryer. "What on Earth—"

"—am I doing here?" Jeff was great at finishing her sentences. That intuitive talent made Frankie believe they were meant to be until reality set in. "I was just about to ask you the same question," he said as a gaggle of young women pushed past him to touch up their makeup in the mirror.

"I, um...heard this place was the happening spot." She paused as she closed the space between them. "I just referred to a nightclub as 'the happening spot'. I think I'm officially old."

They shared a nervous laugh before Jeff jerked his head toward the door. "This place is crazy busy. We can —"

"Yeah, there's a parlor area on the other side."

Jeff smiled. Frankie hadn't seen a smile on his face in months. "Parlor, huh? Yeah, you are getting old."

Frankie gave his shoulder a shove. It felt strange touching him again. She'd given him that shove dozens of times during their short-lived marriage. There was something about touching someone you used to love in a playful manner after enduring the pain of divorce. A strange, foreign quality. Frankie couldn't place it in the moment but it was there.

The two turned out of the noisy bathroom into the parlor. Frankie followed him into the brighter area, looking at fellow clubgoers chat, do lines, and make out in full view. She felt her phone buzz in her pocket and she slipped it out from force of habit.

Where are you?? I'm RTG — this place is Creepsville. Hurry up!

Frankie gave a small chuckle at her phone before typing back that she'd be right out and sliding the cell back in her pocket. She looked back up at Jeff. "Sorry about that. Jen's looking for me. I'm out with her tonight."

"Ah, that explains everything."

Frankie's shoulders dropped. "You have to stop blaming her on us."

Jeff shook his head and leaned against the wall. "I don't blame her."

"Yes, you do." Frankie could feel the warmth of frustration rising in her. The same warmth she'd felt during every mediation leading up to the dissolution of their marriage. "It's not her fault that she's Jake's sister."

The flirtation with Jake began years ago during Frankie's first semester at Yale. She was a freshman and Jake had always been 'Jen's jock older brother' to Frankie. He was three years ahead of her, enjoying his final year as a running back for the Bulldogs. Frankie was a business major who found time to enjoy the occasional raucous campus party in between her studies. The back and forth was harmless tension at first, neither of them thinking it would ever lead to anything. By her junior year, Frankie'd had sex with Jake once in her dorm room, tipsy off of a mix of Schlitz and three shallow puffs of a passed around blunt from a party they'd attended on the floor beneath them. By graduation, Jake was dating his future wife and Frankie had met Jeff.

When Frankie saw Jeff again for the first time at Jen's 30th birthday party, he was rounder and divorced. His new body had turned her on more than she'd cared to admit at the party. As they conversed on a crowded couch in Jen's living room, Frankie knew the sex was inevitable. They waited until the party was over and Jen was passed out drunk in bed before their clothes slid from their bodies. The dirty deed was done before the stroke of midnight. Poor Jen, she had no clue of their past collegiate fling so it never occurred to her that leaving her best friend and her big brother after her party would lead to anything untoward.

But it did, right on Jen's pleather white couch.

"Fine." Jeff rolled his eyes. "It's not her fault, but…"

Frankie watched Jeff search himself for the words. "It's my fault. All me."

"And him." His eyes rose to meet hers. "Are you officially dating him now?"

"Yes."

Pause. "Do you love him?"

"No. I mean, we just got started and—"

"I beg to differ."

Frankie stopped herself from rolling her eyes. "To answer your question, no, we're not at the 'I love you' stage yet."

The sounds of the noisy bathroom drifted in the air before the door closed, silencing the parlor. "So what stage are you two in? Just sex?"

"Jeff, I don't want to talk about this right—"

"Why not?"

Frankie took a deep inhale. Jeff was just as good at finishing her sentences as he was at ending them. "Why does it matter?"

"Because it does." Jeff pushed himself off of the wall and held his head. "Why, Frank?"

The agony in his voice almost convinced Frankie that she'd made the wrong decision in confessing her indiscretion to him a week after Jen's party. He'd cried then, but not because of the cheating. Frankie had followed her confession with a simple statement: "I want a divorce."

It was a shock to all parties involved, as divorce often is. It was particularly stinging once it was revealed who left whom. Guilt wracked Frankie during the mediations. Not because of her betrayal, but because of the tease of freedom. Freedom from a man who seemed perfect on the outside, yes. Jeff was a good provider, and Frankie wanted for nothing.

Nothing but a new life.

"Answer me," Jeff said, his voice elevated. "Just…just tell me why we ended."

Frankie swallowed, her eyes meeting the pleading in his. "I was tired, Jeff, I… I'm not the woman for you. And I'm sorry I didn't realize that before we married, but all I can say is we deserve this."

Jeff's brow furrowed. "We deserve this?" He raised his

palms. "I don't get it, I don't get you."

"We deserve a new start." She felt her gaze drop before she caught herself and looked him square in the eyes. "A new beginning apart from each other. And who knows? Maybe we'll find our way back to each other."

A spark of hope lit up Jeff's face. His lips parted, he paused for a beat. "But maybe we won't."

"Yeah," Frankie said, her voice soft. "Maybe we won't."

Laughs from a group of women behind Jeff punctuated the silence between them. Frankie's eyes darted from the bright light in the parlor back to Jeff. "We'll be okay. This will be scary and new and different… but we'll be okay."

Jeff looked down at his shoes and back at Frankie before spreading his arms. "Come here."

Frankie stepped forward, falling into the arms of the man who loved her, still loved her. And she still loved him, despite her indiscretion. He was scorned but forgiving, or learning to forgive. Frankie had to give him that much.

Frankie slid out of his arms, reaching up on her tiptoes to peck his cheek. "See you around," she whispered before walking toward the exit. She could hear him call for her over the murmur of the crowd but she couldn't look back anymore.

Ross T. Byers

Extruded into this reality during a rare celestial convergence, the entity referred to as Ross T. Byers soon realized that the guise of horror author was the perfect cover while it went about its great and terrible task. It soon patched together a skinsuit and has walked among you ever since, seeding nightmares in the unwary populace through the medium of prose.

Ross T. Byers is also one of the concierges for The Parchment Lounge (the best room!).

Ross T. Byers has established a web presence. If you value your sanity, DO NOT follow him on Twitter @RTByers, or visit his website at www.rosstbyers.com.

One Good Day

Ross T. Byers

I cuffing hate getting locked in car trunks. So why do I keep letting it happen to me? What terrible cuffing life choices do I keep making so I find myself locked in goddamn car trunks again and again? And you want to know what really sucked about this case? Getting locked in another cuffing trunk wasn't even the worst part. The worst part came later.

Now, I know you're thinking, "What the hell, Mateo? How did you wind up in this particular cuffing trunk?" Simple. The woman I love asked me for help.

The morning she came by, I woke up on the floor with a cockroach crawling over my face. I threw it across the room, where it scurried off to the roach metropolis the bastards probably have built beneath my house.

I cuffing hate cockroaches.

I had a real bad hangover that morning, the kind that makes you regret not dying from alcohol poisoning and living to see the sunrise. I spent a minute lying there, thinking about the series of failures that made up my life. Then I got up and shuffled into my living room to hunt through all past dues and final notices for a cigarette to have for breakfast. I found a tequila bottle empty of even the worm, but beside that was a tipped-over beer bottle with a little residue left in it, so I lifted it to my lips and sucked it down. Couldn't find a cigarette, though. I figured it would just be another shitty day when she knocked on my door.

I dragged myself over and opened it, and couldn't help but smile. Natalie looks like some kind of, I don't know, like a Valkyrie. Tall. Blonde. Muscular. Just gorgeous. So, sucker that I am, I let her into my decrepit abode.

"I need your help, Mat," she said.

"Yeah, of course," I said.

She grimaced when my breath hit her face, then put her fists on her hips. "Mateo Rey, you're hungover, aren't you?"

"Hey, you just got here, and already you're using my full name? And so what if I am? I was having a good time with Damian and the gang."

"It's a Wednesday, Mateo! This sort of thing's why I left you."

"Hey, you know that even hungover, I'm still the best." I didn't sit so much as stumble and collapse onto the couch. "And you know I want to help, whatever you need."

She sat in the gray, moth-eaten chair across the coffee table from me and said, "A friend of mine's gone missing. I'm worried about her. I'll pay you, of course."

"No, don't worry about it."

"I insist, Mat. It looks like you need it."

"Alright. I ain't gonna turn down money. Seems like no-one wants to hire a private dick these days."

"Not even that lawyer?"

"I haven't talked to Robert for a few months."

"Well, if I was him, I wouldn't associate with you either." She closed her eyes and sighed. "Sorry. I'm just, God, really stressed right now. I didn't mean it."

Her words felt like a blade twisting in my guts, or maybe that was just the hangover. I waved it off and said, "You'll get your money's worth. I think I'm still licensed, even."

"Well, that's... good."

"So, missing friend. Tell me everything. Tried the police?"

"Hasn't been long enough for them yet."

"But you're worried about her. Why?"

"Amy would never miss a meeting," said Natalie. "She volunteers down at the shelter, teaches self-defense. But it's more than that. She listens, sympathizes, gives us a shoulder. She's important to a lot of women who are way worse off than me. She wasn't there last night, and even the director didn't know why. I kept calling her, but she still won't answer. I'm scared for her, Mat."

"Okay," I said. "Where's she work? Did she show up there?"

"At this bookstore near downtown called The Vault. I called, but I didn't get an answer. Maybe they weren't open."

"What about friends? Family? Who's she hang around with?"

"I know she has a boyfriend, but not how to get in touch with him."

"Okay. I'll try her workplace. See if she's there."

"Thank you, Mat." She pulled out her phone and swiped through it before handing it over to me, saying, "Here's a picture of her."

She was a young Asian woman with short black hair and an easy smile on her lips. Cute, I guess, but not really my type. While I stared, trying to make out the tattoos on her right arm, Natalie wrote me out a check, handing it to me over the crap-strewn table.

"What's this?" I asked.

"Ten percent, up front."

I pocketed the check and offered to make her some coffee, which she declined, then handed back her phone and walked her to the door.

Once she was on the other side of the door, she turned around and said, "Look, Mat, I know you don't want to hear this, but you should really get yourself cleaned up. Maybe think about going to AA. I mean, your life is like a Tom Waits song."

"Who's Tom Waits?"

"He's someone you don't want singing about your life, Mat. Look, at least have a shower and a cup of coffee, for Amy's sake if not your own."

"Sure," I said.

She half-smiled at me, then turned and walked down to her black SUV, which was parked at the curb. I stood in the door and watched her go, shutting the door once she was out of sight.

Coffee would have been nice, but I couldn't afford the grounds, so instead I just jumped into the shower, which was cold despite my cranking the "Hot" knob as far as it would go. Once that was done I threw on my freshest smelling clothes and my leather jacket, in which I found a crushed pack of smokes with two coffin nails still rattling around, but I decided to save them for when the craving got really bad. They were probably the last I would be able to have for a while, even with the check Natalie cut me. I grabbed my camera—it was new, and it was the second-most expensive thing I owned—and pulled up The Vault Bookstore on my phone's GPS. I thought about taking my baby, my customized Shovelhead Electra Glide, which I've put a lot of hours into and love more than my own life, but I was shaky from not having any of the three main staples of my diet—alcohol, caffeine, and nicotine—and didn't want to risk it. So instead I took my nondescript, rusting, nickel-and-diming black panel van.

The bookstore was a good distance away, in the borderland of commercial real estate between the downtown area, the poor and industrial neighborhoods to the east, and the well-to-do neighborhoods and gated communities to the north. So north and a bit west of my house. It was the tail-end of rush hour, so after a hair-raising, road-rage-inducing half-hour traffic thinned out and I was able to make it to the bookstore intact. The show-windows on either side of the door read, "The Vault: New - Used - Rare - Out of Print" in gold, flaking letters. I parked on the street and walked inside, ignoring the meter.

A little bell rang as I stepped in. It was a lot bigger than I thought it would be when standing outside. Most of the surfaces were rich, dark, reddish-brown wood, and even though there were lights everywhere it seemed dim. No one asked if I needed help, and there was nobody behind the register resting on a counter at the back of the room. There was a corridor made by the rows of bookshelves marching from the front of the shop to the back, which gave me a clear line-of-sight to the register. I kept my head on a swivel as I walked slowly down the corridor, peering into the caves made by the bookshelves flanking me on either side. Something about the place creeped me out, and not seeing anybody in those bookshelf spider-holes didn't help.

"May I help you?" asked somebody behind me.

I jumped and spun around, almost tripping over my own feet. The guy standing there had pale blonde hair in a style about a hundred years out of date and eyes like chips of glacial ice, and he was sporting a dusty white suit with a light blue tie.

"Where the cuff did you come from?" I asked, my heart hammering like a piston.

"I was shelving some books. You must have overlooked me."

"Yeah, there's no way that happened."

"It's rather an easy thing to do."

"This place is cuffing creepy, and sneaking up on people really doesn't help. You know that, right?"

"I would appreciate it if you refrained from swearing in my— Wait, did you say 'cuffing?'"

"Sorry," I said. "It's just, you spooked me, is all."

"I apologize, sir. It was not my intention to 'spook' you. Is there anything I can help you with?"

"Yeah, actually. I'm looking for a girl who works here, Amy."

"What is your interest in her? I can't hand out information about employees to just anyone who comes asking, after all," he said.

I pulled a creased, faded card out of my jacket and handed it over, saying, "I'm Mateo Rey, of Rey of Hope Investigations. A friend of Amy's hired me to find her. Seems she's gone missing."

"Hm, well, she certainly should have been here by now, but I haven't seen her yet," said the owner.

"So when was the last time you saw her?"

"Yesterday. I sent her to assess a private collection. She never returned, but I assumed it took the rest of the day and she just went home after. Let me get the address for you."

The pale man walked to the counter and scribbled down something on a piece of paper, which he brought back to me.

"Amy is quite dear to me," said the man as he handed me the address. "Almost like a daughter. If she is in trouble, I would greatly appreciate if you could extricate her from it."

Our fingers brushed as I took the paper from him, and I shuddered. It was like touching frozen wax.

"Yeah, of course," I said, punching the address into my phone. It told me to go to one of the nicest neighborhoods in the city, way up on the northern edge of town. The paper also had a name on it: Lester Hammond.

"Well, thanks for your help," I said, walking away. I just wanted out of there.

"Good luck," said the pale man behind me.

I turned around to say something cocky, you know, like "I don't need luck, I've got skill," or something, but he was gone, like he'd never been there. So, being the sensible dick I am, I ran out the door.

The Hammond mansion was an older one, all slate gray and gloomy, squatting in the middle of an acre of lawn. A tall privacy hedge rose up all around the property, and I could see two towers rising above the cobwebbed foliage, pointing up at the sky like a bruja's fingers, as though to curse it. The only break in the hedge was the mouth of the wide, curving driveway. There was a black wrought-iron gate, but it was open. So, it seemed easy to get in, but I could tell by the size of the property and the neighborhood that he would have goons. Rich assholes always have goons, and I hate goons. I hate them because they do things like lock me in cuffing car trunks.

I didn't think I had a chance of getting inside. How many rich pricks can you think of who would let in a strange brown man? But this was for Natalie, so I drove my utter-crap-mobile through the open gate and up to the big house. No one came up to question or assault me, so I walked up to the door and rang the bell. I stood there for a few moments before an older guy in an expensive-looking leisure suit opened the door. I put on my most charming smile and held out my hand for a shake.

"Hello, sir. My name's Mateo Rey, of Rey of Hope Investigations. I'm looking for Lester Hammond."

"Do you have any identification?" he asked.

"Of course," I said, digging my wallet out of my jeans. I showed him my P.I. license, and he leaned forward to read it, squinting. When he was done, he straightened up and shook my hand.

"I'm Lester Hammond," he said. "What may I help you with?"

"I have a few questions to ask you, if you don't mind," I said.

"Not at all," said Hammond. "I don't get much company since my wife passed. Please, come inside."

"I'm sorry to hear about your wife," I said as we

walked down the wide, oak-paneled, art-strewn main hall.

"Thank you," he said. "It was a sudden thing. Bone cancer. Didn't find it in time. Doctors aren't infallible, you know. It's been about, oh, six months now since she left me."

"Life is shit," I said.

"Indeed it is," he said, opening a door to our right and gesturing me inside. "This is where I prefer to entertain visitors."

It was the creepiest cuffing room I'd ever seen, and I'd just left what had to be the creepiest bookshop on Earth. The room was lined with shelves made of dark wood, which were filled with big, old books and beetles in glass display cases, pinned to felt beds. It was cuffing beetles everywhere, big ones and little ones and colorful ones and plain ones and ones that looked like they would bite your eyes out while you slept and others that looked like they would crawl in your ear and eat your brain. It made me wish I'd just stayed on the floor beside my bed that morning. Then again, at least there weren't any cockroaches.

I sat in a faded green overstuffed chair, and he sat in a similar one beside me. There was a small, round table between us, and he pulled a cigar out of an inscribed box lying on it. He offered it to me, so of course I took it, trying to hide my excitement at the chance to have some quality tobacco. He lit my cigar with a match, then his own, puffing contentedly on it for a minute before speaking.

"So, what questions did you want to ask me?"

"At the moment, where did you get such a fine cigar?"

"Brazil."

"Hot damn. What were you doing there?"

"Collecting," he said, gesturing about the room. "There are many unique specimens that can be found in South America, especially around the Amazon."

I nodded, trying not to look at the beetles, which of

course didn't work since they were everywhere. Even the table had a beetle design carved into its surface. So I just tried to focus on him and let the rest of the room melt into a peripheral haze.

"So, I want to ask about a woman who came by yesterday to look at your books."

"Oh, yes, Amy," said Hammond. "Delightful young woman."

"Yeah," I said. "So, she did come by."

"She did. I showed her this very room. Most of my books are in here. I have an extensive collection of rare and antique entomological treatises, you know. It's the envy of several collectors."

"And you were thinking of selling it to The Vault?"

"Part of it, if their offer was reasonable."

"Do you really think a little bookshop like that could afford it?"

"You never know," said Hammond. "I've heard the owner is quite... resourceful."

"Okay," I said. "So, she came by to check out your collection."

"Yes, and then she left."

"Do you know where she went once she was done?"

"No. I assume back to the bookshop."

"Owner says she never showed up after leaving for here."

"My, that's ominous," said Hammond. "I'm sorry, Mr. Rey. All I know is she left sometime in the afternoon, between three and four, I think. Jeopardy! was on, which I watch diligently."

"So she didn't tell you where she was going?"

"No, but she thanked me for my time and told me I'd hear about an offer soon. Would you like some coffee?"

"Yeah, that would be great, thanks," I said.

"I think there's some still in the pot. I'll be right back."

Hammond left, and I laid the smoldering stub of the cigar in a thick, ceramic ashtray by the cigar box. Sick of all those dead beetles staring at me, I looked down at the carpet, which is why I spotted a thin black strap poking out in a loop from beneath my chair. I reached down and tugged on it. A small black handbag slid out between my feet. I picked it up and went through it. The I.D. in the handbag was issued to, you guessed it, Amy Wu, and the face in the picture matched the one Natalie had shown me earlier. I stuffed the I.D. back in the handbag and stood up, hoping to get out of there quietly, when Hammond came in through the door, a steaming mug of coffee in each hand.

"You aren't leaving, are you? I have your coffee right here."

"I changed my mind. Don't want my acid reflux to flare up, you know?"

"Of course," said Hammond. "What's that you have there?"

"Amy's purse," I said, figuring lying was useless at that point.

"Oh, my, where did you find it?"

"Under my chair."

"Well, she must have dropped it while looking at my books."

"She must have," I said, hoping I looked and sounded like I believed his lie. I still felt hung-over, so I was worried my acting chops weren't up to snuff. "I'll just take it with me for when I catch up with her."

"Of course," said Hammond. "I wouldn't want to keep it from her."

"Well, I'm going to go chase after her," I said. "I know she has a boyfriend. Maybe he knows something."

"Maybe he does," said Hammond, backing out of the way as I walked towards the door. "I certainly hope you find her."

"Thanks for all your help," I said as I walked past. "I can find the door myself; you just stay and enjoy your coffee."

"Goodbye, Mr. Rey."

"Yeah, see you around," I said.

I hurried down the hall, the handbag slapping against my thigh with every other step. I planned to go straight to the police with it and my suspicions and let them deal with things. I opened the front door and came face-to-chest with a goon I immediately and lovingly dubbed Big Gringorilla. He folded his arms across his chest and frowned down at me.

I put up my fists, purse dangling from my elbow, and said, "I was an Army Ranger, pendejo. You really want to mess with me?"

"No," he said. "I'm just distracting you so he can get behind you."

"Acho men," I said, pain blooming behind my eyes and stars exploding in my vision as I dropped into unconsciousness. Hey, even the best combat training in the world doesn't save you from a sucker punch.

My next oh-so-wonderful conscious experience was waking up in the cuffing car trunk, feeling more hung-over than ever, though the shot to the skull I took probably had something to do with that. From my near inability to move and the way I was wedged inside so my left arm was trapped beneath me and had fallen asleep at some point, I judged I was in some tiny, eco-cuffing-friendly car trunk. Whichever goon was driving hit a pot-hole, slamming my head against the lid and sending a wave of pain from the tender back of my skull around to my eyes. I couldn't wait to get out, but at the same time I dreaded it.

The car shuddered and ground to a halt on what felt like gravel. I tried to prepare myself for some half-assed escape attempted, but all my muscles were cramped up. I heard the car doors open and slam, and footsteps in the gravel. The trunk opened, and I saw that Big Gringorilla was accompanied by Bigger Gringorilla. They grabbed me by the arms and pulled me out of the trunk. We were parked in a deserted lot, a sagging chain-link fence along two sides, including the one that bordered the river. They hauled me along, my legs barely long enough for my toes to drag through the gravel. Once we were in the center of the lot, they threw me down to the rocks. I stayed down, watching them, cautious, but they just stood there, staring at me, so I got up slowly.

"Not so rough, fellas, this is real leather," I said, brushing the dust off my jacket.

They exchanged a look, then went back to staring at me. Bigger Gringorilla pulled my camera from underneath his windbreaker, holding it up so I could see it.

"Yeah, that's my camera," I said. "It's not like I took any pictures."

Bigger dropped it to the gravel and stomped it to pieces.

"Oh, come on, man. That thing was expensive!"

Big Gringorilla pulled my phone out of his pocket.

"Yeah, okay, I get it," I said. "I didn't take pictures with that either. Can I please have it back?"

Big turned and tossed it over the chain-link into the weeds on the other side.

"Mothercuffer!" I yelled, and charged him, regretting it immediately as he turned on a dime and snapped a jab into my jaw. I stumbled back, the gravel crunching beneath my boots. Bigger just stood behind his partner, watching. He looked bored.

"Damn," I said, tasting blood from my loosened molars, and spat into the gravel.

"Mr. Hammond doesn't like strangers coming around asking questions," said Big.

"Yeah, I got that," I said. "I'll make sure to stay away. We done here?"

"Not yet." Big cracked his knuckles.

"Sorry, pal," said Bigger. "It's part of the job. I just want you to know it's in no way a racial thing."

"Now that you've said that, I kind of think it is."

"No, seriously," said Bigger. "I'm not a racist. I voted

for Obama both times! Brown is beautiful."

"Lo que me estàs diciendo es digno de ser emitido por tu culo."

"Shut the hell up," said Big Gringorilla, and punched me in the other side of my face.

I tried to fight back, but it was two-on-one and I was still hungover. Pretty soon, they had me on the ground. Then Big kicked me, so I curled up as best I could. It wasn't long before my stomach rebelled and I vomited bile and tequila all over Big Gringorilla's shoes and pants. Both goons jumped away from me, making disgusted sounds. The cuts inside my mouth burned, and the powerful aroma of tequila wafted up from the puddle of puke.

"He yakked on my goddamn Nikes," said Big Gringorilla, pulling the soaked hems of his trousers away from his shoes, the half-digested worm lying limp and curled on top of his right foot.

I couldn't help but smile at that.

"We should kill him," said Big.

"We're not killing him," said Bigger.

"But Mr. Hammond said—"

"I don't care what Mr. Hammond said. I'm not going to become a murderer just because he says so, and I won't be a party to murder, either. Besides, look at him. He gets the message. You get the message, right, guy?"

"It's painfully clear," I said.

"You're funny," said Bigger Gringorilla. "That's good. Don't lose that."

Big Gringorilla rolled me on my stomach and pulled my wallet from back pocket.

"You're paying for my shoes, asshole," he said.

"Oh, c'mon, don't be a douche," I said, staring up at him with the one eye that would stay open.

He looked at Bigger Gringorilla, who shrugged. So he extracted the measly sum of cash and dropped my wallet in the puddle of tequila-bile. They left without another word, walking back to their silver Prius, Bigger folding into the driver's side. The tires pelted me with bits of gravel as the hybrid pulled away. I rolled over onto my side to get away from the smell of my own puke. A cockroach crawled over the gravel, not far from my face, so I spat blood at it.

After lying there for a bit, catching my breath, I forced myself to my feet. I picked my wallet out of the tequila-bile and tried to wipe it off on the gravel, which didn't really work, but I stuck it back in my jeans anyway. Then came the unpleasant task of hobbling around the fence in search of my phone. It wasn't hard to find, and, in my first bit of good luck all day, it still worked and didn't look much worse than before. I didn't have the money for a cab, so I called the only person I could think of.

"Hello?"

"Hey, Natalie," I said, trying not to sound like I'd been run through a meat-grinder. "I know this may be a lot to ask, but could you give me a ride?"

"Too drunk to drive?"

"No, just beaten and left to die."

"Uh-huh. And where are you?"

"I don't actually know. Some empty lot down by the river."

"And where do you need to go?"

"Oh, probably the hospital, but since I can't afford that, I guess back to this rich prick's place."

She sighed. "Find me a street name and I'll come get you."

I groaned at the thought of more walking, but said, "Sure."

***

I was sitting on a cinder-block at the nearest corner, smoking my second-to-last cigarette, when Natalie pulled up in her black SUV. I forced myself up and hobbled over.

"Thanks," I said as I slid into her passenger seat.

24

"You're sure you don't want to go to the hospital?" she asked, eyeing me up and down.

"Yeah, I'm sure. So, I've got good news and bad news."

"Lay it on me," she said.

"Well, I think I found Amy—"

"Where is she?" asked Natalie.

"Yeah, that's the bad news. I'm pretty sure she's at this rich asshole's house, but I don't know if she's alive or not."

"Where?" she asked, her face grim. The last time I'd seen that expression on her, she'd beaten this meat-head biker unconscious with a pool cue. She was so hot. I love it when she gets all action-heroine-y. I would have put some moves on her if I wasn't in an incredible amount of pain.

"Look, maybe we shouldn't just charge in," I said. "The asshole's got goons. Maybe we should just go to the police, let them deal with it."

"No police," said Natalie. "Where's my friend, Mat?"

"I'll tell you, but you're not going in alone."

"What, you think you're coming with me?"

"Every step of the way."

"Mat, you can't even walk right now."

"I'll be fine by the time we get there. C'mon, Nat. I have to see this through to the end, you know?"

Natalie shook her head, sighed, and said, "Why do I always fall for your bullshit? Fine, come along and die from internal bleeding if you want. Now where is she?"

I pulled up the route on my phone, and we took off. It wasn't the most pleasant car ride I've ever had, not just because of the excruciating pain but also because she likes country. Still, it was better than the cuffing car trunk. I had her pull over when we were still a block-and-a-half away from Hammond's mansion.

"You still got that Louisville Slugger in here?" I asked.

"I've got better than that," she said, lifting the edge of

her leather jacket to show me the butt of her Sig Sauer .45, nestled cozily in a shoulder holster.

"Oh, Nat, put that away. No guns."

"What? Oh, come on Mat, don't be a gun-shy pansy."

"Dios, you know I'm not gun-shy. But look around. This is a really nice neighborhood. Someone will hear the shot and call the police. And, unlike in my neighborhood, they'll be here—" I snapped my fingers "—like that. You know, I'm not even packing."

"What? Why not? Where's your gun?"

"Well, I, ah, I pawned it."

"You pawned your gun? Wasn't that your service pistol?"

"Yeah, well, I had no cash and I needed booze."

"Jesus, Mat. You need a gun. Your work's dangerous."

"I'm a private dick—"

"Oh my God, you need to stop calling yourself that."

"Most of the time, I'm just following cheating assholes and taking pictures of them in flagrante. Look, we're way off topic. Just take the bat. I've got a plan."

"You've got a plan?"

"Oh, yeah."

***

I limped around the privacy hedge and up Hammond's driveway. Big Gringorilla spotted me right away and jogged over. I noticed he was wearing new, cheap shoes.

"You've gotta be kidding," he said.

"No need to panic," I said, waving my hands to show they were empty. "I just came by to get my van."

"Yeah, well it's gone. Wilbur's driving it to the dump as we speak. It was a piece of shit."

"Wait, your big friend's name is Wilbur?" I asked, circling around him. He kept his eyes on me, turning his back to the street.

"We're not fr—"

I threw a weak jab at him, but he slapped it away and crushed my nose into my face. My back slammed to the pavement, and I swear I felt a rib dig into my lung.

"Stupid wetback. Trying to get even for that beating I laid on you?"

I wanted to say, "No, I was just distracting you so she could get behind you," but all that came out was a pained wheeze. And besides, I think the crack of Natalie's bat against the back of his skull said it better than I could've. He tipped forward and face-planted in the driveway with a splat. I grabbed Natalie's proffered hand and she pulled me up.

"He was going to kill you," she said.

"Yeah, but I knew you had my back."

"I had to run to get here in time."

"Sure, but you made it."

"You're a dick."

"Funny," I said. "I love word-play."

She groaned and said, "Let's just get inside."

We walked up to the door, Natalie gripping her bat tight enough to make it creak. I turned the doorknob, and the door swung open.

"Who keeps their door unlocked?" she asked.

I shrugged. She stepped past me and took point inside, baseball bat raised and ready to strike. I limped after her. I was worried some more of Hammond's goons might pop out at us, but none did. Apparently, he only had the two, but the man himself stepped into the hallway to greet us.

"What's going on here?" he asked, his tone demanding, but he froze when he saw my face.

"Good evening, Lester," I said. "So, where are you keeping Amy?"

"I don't know what—"

Natalie smashed her bat down on his shoulder. He dropped to his knees, mouth agape, howling. Then she punched him in the face, which shut his mouth.

"Where's Amy, cocksucker?" she asked, pressing the bat against his ear.

"B-basement."

"Take us there," she said.

"It's through here," said Hammond, standing slowly, clutching his shoulder. He led us down the hall and into the goddamn beetle room, and it was no less creepy than the first cuffing time. The place put me on edge, making me wish for the comforting weight of an M4 in my hands, but all I had was my own busted-up self. Fat lot of good that had done me so far. I saw Amy's bag was now on the table with the cigars, on display like it was one of his beetles.

Hammond pulled a key out of his pants pocket and unlocked a door hiding in the shadows between two bookshelves. It opened on a narrow set of stairs, flanked on both sides by stone, which descended into darkness. It felt like I was looking down a lion's throat.

"Oh, you are so going first," I told Hammond.

He did, still clutching his shoulder. Natalie followed, and I brought up the rear. I kept looking back at the door, expecting it to shut on its own, like in some cheap horror flick. It didn't, but I didn't feel any easier, either.

Hammond hit a switch that lit up the long fluorescent tubes hanging from the ceiling. The stairs let out on a small room with rough stone walls. There was some cobwebbed crap in one corner. Directly across from us was a door that looked damn near ancient. It was made of wood and banded with iron.

"Amy is through here," he said, producing another key, unlocking the door, and pulling it open.

The ceiling and walls of the corridor beyond were rounded, and made of the same rough stone as the first room. It was more like a tunnel than a man-made passage, sloping gradually away from us into darkness. Bare bulbs hung from the ceiling at irregular intervals, shedding dim yellow light. Hammond led us down it, our footsteps echoing off the walls, which grew damper the deeper we went. The door plugging the end of the tunnel was the twin of the door at the beginning. He had to pause and unlock it, too.

The chamber beyond was massive. Ahead of us, in the center of the chamber, was an enormous, apparently bottomless pit. The wall around the pit was studded with alcoves gouged into the stone, flat iron bars covering their mouths, making them cages, pens. Most were empty, some had human bones jumbled on the floor, and the two nearest us had women locked inside. In the cage on the left was Amy, clothed in jeans and a Franz Ferdinand tee-shirt. In the other cage was an emaciated woman lying in the fetal position, her long, brown hair fanning out around her. She was wearing a short dress and earrings.

Amy grabbed the bars of the cage and said, "Natalie! You need to get us out of here, quick. Bethany's been here a while, and she needs help really bad. She just collapsed a few minutes ago."

"The hell is wrong with you, man?" I said. "Get them out of there!"

Natalie grabbed a fistful of his hair and hauled him over to Amy's cage, slamming his face into the bars. A thin trail of blood trickled from beneath Natalie's fingers. More blood dribbled from his nose and lips.

"We must not disrupt the sacrifice," he said, his esses whistling through the new gap in his teeth.

"Get. Her. Out."

"But we'll all die!" shouted Hammond.

Natalie slammed his face into the bars again.

"Okay, okay, okay," said Hammond, yanking the key out of his pocket and sticking it in the lock. It shrieked as he turned it. Natalie threw Hammond aside and nearly ripped the door off its hinges. Amy jumped out, stretched, then hugged Natalie.

"Oh my God, thank you, Nat," she said. "I can't

believe I let myself get damselled like that."

"Don't worry about it," said Natalie, hugging her back. "I'm just glad you're safe."

"Asshole drugged the coffee he gave me. I haven't touched a thing he's given me since. But she did," said Amy, looking over at her fellow prisoner – Bethany, I guess – lying still in her cage.

I really didn't like the sound of that. Natalie yanked the key out of the lock and ran over to the other cage. Hammond sat up, groaning, and Amy walked over to him.

"Usually, I try to avoid violence," she said, then kicked him in the gut. He chuffed and fell to his side.

"I've gotta say, though, that felt really good," she said, flashing a wicked grin at me.

"Hey, don't kill him," I said.

"I'm not killing him," she said. "Merely thanking him for locking me in a cage."

I gave her the most skeptical look I could muster, then looked over to Natalie, who was kneeling over the other captive woman. I was no medic, but I still thought I might be able to help, so I shuffled over and hunkered down next to Natalie, my shoulder brushing hers. I touched the woman's arm, her skin fever-hot and quivering. Then she opened her dark-circled eyes and screamed, her body convulsing, back arching against the stone floor.

"We need to go!" yelled Amy as Natalie shouted "What's happening?" and the woman kept screaming. Hammond started wheezing, but I think he was trying to scream, too. Then the woman's flesh bulged, everywhere, quivering lumps rising up along her arms and face and legs and beneath her dress. There were tearing, popping sounds, and blood splashed the floor. And with it came the cockroaches, crawling out from underneath her dress, tearing their way through her skin, wet and red. One crawled out of her slack, open mouth. She had stopped screaming.

The swarm of roaches fled away from us and over the

lip of the pit, out of sight and into the dark where they belong. They left faint streaks of red behind.

"What the cuff was that?" I said, turning to glare at Hammond.

The world tilted. Natalie and I stumbled into each other, and she kept me from falling. Hammond slid towards the pit, but didn't go in. A cacophonous, dry rumbling emanated from the hole, like a rock-slide whispering. Hammond wheeze-screamed and tried to crawl away. Two whipping, colossal, cockroach antennae sprouted from the pit and bent against the arching stone ceiling. I wheeled Natalie back towards the door and shoved her, yelling, "Run!"

"Grgzglthyzzk is coming!" screamed Hammond from the floor.

Amy was already sprinting up the tunnel. Natalie was at the nearest door. A hissing horde of cockroaches, some as long as a foot, crawled over the lip of the pit and advanced on us. I saw the armored, rounded brown tip of the roachzilla's head appear above the rim of the pit. It seemed to go on forever, like I was staring into a black-hole's event horizon.

So I high-tailed it. Hammond quickly gained his feet and, since his ribs were whole, caught up to me. Amy was standing with one hand on the door at the other end of the tunnel, rocking up and down on her toes. Natalie made it through the door, but we were far behind. Running was incredibly painful, and Hammond was panting beside me.

"Grgzglthyzzk demands sacrifice," he wheezed.

I knew the hungry cockroach horde was right on our heels, about to catch and eat us, so I did the thing any heroic dick would do and elbowed Hammond in the face. He stumbled away from me into the stone wall of the tunnel, but didn't fall. Still, I hoped the cockroaches would pause long enough while devouring him for me to make it through the door. Then I heard the persistent bastard start running again behind me, so even though it hurt like hell I put my head down and sprinted. I collapsed once I was through, but rolled over to see Natalie smash Hammond's face with her bat. He fell back into the tunnel, and the cockroaches were on him. Amy slammed the door before any could get through. Hammond screamed. Even through the thick, old door, I could hear him. It seemed to go on forever. Sometimes, when I close my eyes, I can still hear him, like he was never allowed to stop screaming and it goes on, eternally, just at the edge of my hearing.

"Natalie..." I didn't really know what to say, so I lifted myself off the floor.

"He deserved it," she said.

We both looked at Amy. She shrugged and said, "The roach god demanded sacrifice, right?"

"Sure," I said. "So, why isn't it, you know, smashing buildings and destroying the city?"

The young woman shrugged again. "Maybe it was appeased."

"Let's get out of here," said Natalie.

Amy grabbed her bag from that damn beetle room as we left, and once we were outside the mansion I was struck by how normal everything was. The same overcast sky. The same privacy hedge. The same Big Gringorilla unconscious in the driveway. The same Wilbur, AKA Bigger Gringorilla, standing at the edge of the driveway, looking from his sprawled-out partner to the three of us, mouth agape. We stared back. He turned around and walked away, whistling, to disappear behind the other side of the privacy hedge. Yeah, everything exactly like it was, as if a colossal cockroach with a gibberish name hadn't crawled out of the bowels of the Earth.

"That... That did really just happen, right?" I asked, turning to the women beside me. "I mean, it's not the DTs or something, right?"

"Nope, it really happened," said Amy.

"'Man, I really hoped it was just DTs." I held out my hand. "I'm Mat."

"Mat? Oh! It's nice to finally meet you," said Amy, shaking my hand and smiling. "Nat's told me a lot about you."

"Don't say that," said Natalie. "He'll get ideas."

I laughed, shaking out my last cigarette, and saw Amy staring at it.

"Hey, could I bum that? I could really use a smoke."

My last damn cigarette, so of course, sucker that I am, I gave it to her and lit it. I dropped the empty pack on Hammond's lawn, and we walked down the driveway, heading for Natalie's SUV.

"So, would you guys call what happened in there Lovecraftian?" asked Amy, smoke drifting from her mouth. "It definitely wasn't Kafka-esque

"Um, what?" I asked.

"I'd say it was horrible," said Natalie.

"Yeah, it was." Amy's smile disappeared for a moment, and she muttered, "I hate occultists."

Then her smile sprang back and she said, "At least there weren't any tentacles this time."

"This time?" I asked.

"So do you want a ride, Amy?" asked Natalie.

"Yeah, that would be great. It's a long walk back home from here."

"Wait," I said. "What did you mean by, 'this time'?"

"I can drop you back off at your place after we get Mat to the hospital."

"Yeah, I should probably shower before heading to work. Think my boss'll be mad?"

"Really, I'm kinda freaked out you said that. Shit like this has happened before?"

"Just get in the car, Mat," said Natalie.

"Yeah, alright," I said, and slid into the passenger seat. I probably would have been better off in the back, but I wanted to sit next to Natalie.

Amy got in behind me and laid down, saying, "I'm going to take a nap, guys. Wake me when we get there."

Natalie got behind the wheel and slammed the door. I turned my head towards her.

"You know, this is it. I'm done. This P.I. shit has gotten way too weird for me. Damian still wants me to work at his shop, so from here on out I'm a mechanic. And AA. AA is probably good."

"I think that would be good for you, Mat."

"So does the hero get a kiss?"

She looked at me, and I stared into her beautiful, bright blue eyes. Then she turned away and stared down the road.

"Not this time," she said, and drove.

Leslie Kung

Leslie Kung is a Chinese American author whose family holds the Guinness world record for longest recorded genealogy. In between parenting and adjusting her clever human disguise, she writes a variety of fiction, all enriched with cultural, social and experiential depth. She resides in Iowa with three small humans, one leopard gecko, and a mysteriously self-sustaining tank of guppies.

Kung is the concierge for The Cedar Room and deeply enjoys supporting other writers.

Find her on Facebook:
https://www.facebook.com/AuthorLHKung/
Become a patron to read more:
https://www.patreon.com/ArtemisRising
Follow her on Twitter:
https://twitter.com/misshybridvigor
Follow her on Amazon:
https://www.amazon.com/Leslie-Kung/e/B01AIL7DEG

The Night She Began

Leslie Kung

Carolinas, 70's

The moths tapped rhythmically against the dusty glass, attracted to the glow of the lantern bulb. Their fluttering wings cast strobing shadows over the Spanish moss hanging from the old oak trees. The ground beneath Beula's feet squelched as she walked further into the swamp. Mama told her over and over again never to go into the swamp their house backed up to, especially never at night, or she'd take a switch to her behind, but this— THIS was different. The bottoms of her only bell bottom jeans, the ones she'd saved up her own money for, were soaked now, and she'd been running for what felt like hours. Though the air was thick with moisture, her mouth felt dry. Streaks of tears added to the moisture gathering on her dark brow.

Beula was darker brown than all her cousins and teased for it. But no matter how much they made fun of her, right now she'd give anything to be safe at home on the bottom bunk under Carmine who threw things at her head when the lights went off. Carmine was twelve years old—two years older than her, and though cruel at times, might have a better idea of what to do lost in the muck, stuck out in the dark with 'skeeters trying to suck her dry and the gleam of eyes reflecting back from the electric lantern.

A sound. A cracking of underbrush. Beula swung around, the lantern light doing a crazy Soul Train lightshow across the expanse of roots and dark water. She was knee deep in the cold, gripping wet now. The night air pressed down on her sweat laden curls, and she looked back and forth, heart pounding.

And the memory wouldn't leave her.

The men who came up to the house, pounding on the door.

The shouts and jeers.

The brick shattering the window.

Her mama, pushing her out the back door and whispering "Run, girl. Run, and don't you dare stop runnin —"

The screams.

The light from fire. From torches.

The shadows of peaked masks, holes cut for black voids where should have been eyes.

And then the dogs barked, and they came tromping through, screaming "One's getting away!" And she ran and ran.

But the noise didn't turn into anything. No hooded figures, no lengths of rope. No dogs. She clutched her chest and whispered a prayer that was unintelligible even to herself. She was lost now, but if there was a God, she would not be found. Not by men in sheets. Not by gators.

Beula took a deep breath, slapped away another greedy insect, and did the scariest, smartest thing she'd ever been called upon to do: She turned off her electric lantern and continued onward, letting the humid darkness swallow her whole.

Deliver Me

Leslie Kung

South Korea, 2018

Sun Jae parked his motorbike on the curb and unhooked his delivery box. He flicked his thumb over his phone screen again, checking the address. Somewhere in this office building he was supposed to deliver five pizzas. Not bothering to remove his helmet, he shouldered open the glass door and ascended to the third floor, skipping the elevator in favor of long, leaping strides over three to four steps at a time.

"Three zero nine," he muttered to himself, as he reached the right floor and depressed the push bar on the door with the edges of the pizza boxes. When he stepped into the empty corridor, he realized that everything was dark, except for the ambient security lights that never turned off. The tint on his helmet visor was just dark enough to make it difficult to even see, so he flipped it up with the edge of his thumb.

The slide of aerodynamic plastic and the click of his helmet visor locking into open position was the loudest sound. He looked quickly back and forth, the heat from the insulated pizza box starting to seep into his hand and side.

"Hello?" he called out. "Someone ordered pizza? Hello?"

There was no answer. There was no movement. Sun

Jae started to curse to himself.

"Wrong floor, wrong room. Or it's a prank, and I'm paying for these. Damn."

He pulled out his phone and called the customer's number to double check the address, ready to use a restrained and polite voice. On his end, the phone started to ring as he shouldered his way back through the stair access door.

Before he was all the way in the landing, he heard it behind him: a cell phone ringing.

He turned around, waiting, his eyes narrowed. The ringing went to an operator's voice saying the person he was calling wasn't available. And the high-pitched bell tones somewhere on this floor also stopped.

With a terrible feeling, he ventured back into the dark hall.

"Excuse me? Is someone here? I have the pizza delivery…" He thumbed down on his screen, and pressed the flashlight function, illuminating a small circle of mass produced, thin carpeting with pixel-y color blocks.

Then he switched screens and pressed redial, not even holding the phone to his ear. He could hear the ringtone clearly enough in the otherwise oppressive silence of the abandoned office building. Three rings in, just as before, the bell tones of someone's cell phone started up.

Sun Jae carefully put the pizza down on the counter of the reception desk in the main entry and walked further into the darkness. Glass doors lined the hall, each room empty as he passed them, except for the hint of night sky through windows and the lurking shapes of inert office furniture.

Nearly at the end of the hall, he heard the cell phone clearly to the left before the operator voice informed him that the other person must not be available. He hung up before it got to voicemail again. The ringing from the room to the left also stopped.

Sun Jae turned off the flashlight function, tucking his

phone back into the back pocket of his jeans. He put a hand on the contact plate mounted on the glass door and gently pushed in. It swung open with no resistance, and he felt his heart rate kick up a few notches.

"Excuse me? Is someone here? I have the pizzas you ordered…" He found himself speaking in a voice quieter than his usual as he surveyed the office before him. There was a cell phone on the desk, and an open purse. His eyes followed the trail of obviously spilled items to a tube of lipstick on the floor beside the desk… Where he spotted a leg and foot protruding from under the desk, heel hanging out of a shiny patent polka dot flat.

Sun Jae screamed, jumping back.

The leg jerked and there was a resounding gong-like bang as the person under the desk sat up and banged their head into the metal underside.

"HEY!" screamed an angry, high voice.

"Aaahhh!" Sun Jae banged his back into the edge of the glass door.

"What the hell!" said the voice from beneath the desk.

"Oh my god, you scared me!" he shrieked, before he capped his hands over his mouth.

"I don't have anything to steal! I'm calling the cops! I have a weapon!"

The foot had pulled back under the desk, but manicured fingers crept up, hands frantically patting around, knocking the purse over further.

"Your phone is in the MIDDLE of the desk, you crazy…" said Sun Jae, clutching his chest. "And I WILL BE THE ONE calling the police, lady! Who the hell orders pizza and goes to sleep in the dark like this?!"

The hands slid further and fingers nudged into the cell phone. Like an octopus, her fingers wrapped around and pulled it back into her cave.

"I'm turning on the lights, and you're gonna pay me, and I'm LEAVING. You gave me a heart attack!"

"What pizza?! I don't know what you're… Oh my

god, what time is it? Where is everyone?"

As Sun Jae felt along the walls by the entry and flipped on the light, a tousled, bleary-eyed head poked up from behind the desk, like a poorly controlled hand puppet. Glasses on upside down, the crazy lady glared at him like he was in the wrong. With his hand still fisted in the fabric of the hoodie over his heart, he glared right back.

The light illuminated the messy office, along with a series of notes on printer paper, written in lipstick. Both of them noticed the three sheets on top of the desk at the same time. As Sun Jae walked closer, he could see a few words like "b*tch" and "stole." He paced closer, craning his head as the woman leaned over the desk with her hands pressed flat and went pale.

"I'm so sorry. This is... Someone used my phone." She gathered all the papers and turned them over before he got a better look. "Pizzas, you said? I'll pay for them. I'm sorry..."

"This was a prank, wasn't it?"

"It's nothing. What's the total? Where are the pizzas?"

Sun Jae looked at her, her braid half falling out, blouse untucked. He took in the tremble of her lips and her helpless glance at the mess and let out a long breath before pulling his helmet off to push dark brown hair away from his sweaty brow.

He was going to pay for the pizzas after all.

Beginning Again: Homecoming

Leslie Kung

Expanded world and story published in Dark Space *by Elm Books under the title "Lazarus Squad".*

United Federation, 3001

Long-shifters, street vendors, and school children would usually be stepping off the evening shuttle, but not today. The landing pad and ped-mall were eerily quiet, an old holiday called 'Veteran's Day,' recently revived by the United Fed.

A few family members of servicemen waited with reddened eyes, standing isolated even from each other. A small group of protesters frowned and projected holo-signs from their Y-coms: "DEATH-CHEATERS GO BACK" and "CY-TRASH NOT WELCOME!" Hostile expressions and tense postures put a dangerous edge to the homecoming.

Dantilly clutched her mother's hand. From ankle to cheek, she was pressed against her mother's biofabric jumpsuit. She flinched when the shuttle doors phased clear with an electric sounding whine, turning her face into her mother's thigh.

"Tilly, look! Daddy's coming home!" Her mother's voice was soft but strong enough to be heard over the shouting.

"Go back to your charging docks, perverts!"

In the last rays of evening sun, her mother's hair shone like polished wood grain on an artifact she'd seen behind a museum case on Halifax Station. She looked up into her mother's brown eyes, checked the relaxed curve of her lips, and darted a nervous glance toward the transport. Figures emerged from the large shuttle.

A woman limped slowly at the forefront of the group, wearing iFatigues, which everyone called "iTeegs," in their dormant dark green. Dantilly stared at her with wide eyes. Though the protesters threw holographic refuse at her and jeered, she didn't even flinch. Dantilly didn't think she looked like a cyborg. She just looked tired. No one was there to meet her.

"Bio-humans before Frankensteins!"

Behind the woman, two men emerged. One was clutching a military issue brimmed hat, trying to cover his face with a cupped hand and raised forearm. His taller companion walked in front of him, staying between his friend and the angry sign holders.

One of the protesters threw a holo of a drone soldier ready to fire right in front of the men. The tall friend spasmodically threw up his hands. Lines of energy traced between his fingers. Almost immediately, he shook his hands out like he was flicking water off his fingertips, dismissing the charges. The protesters screamed in response.

"CYBORGS, GET OUT!"

"Live weapons! Civ code violations! They shouldn't be here!"

"He's going to fry us all. They're not human anymore!"

They pushed forward in a wave, outnumbering the few family and friends who came to welcome the soldiers home, and formed a ring around the two veterans. From the shuttle, a few more men and women in iTeegs stepped out, hands fisted, and jaws clenched. The circle of protesters broke and receded as the soldiers sidled up and put their backs together. The man with the cap on slowly stood up straighter as he pulled the hat off.

Dantilly gave a small shout as she saw her daddy. He looked the same, only half his face was covered in silvery flash circuits. The eye on that side looked a bit funny. Her mother had explained it to her several times, so she would be ready. It was called 'bio-ware,' and it saved daddy's life. His hair was still blue-black, and his skin was still golden bronze, just like her own. Even with his angry face on, he didn't look scary to her.

"Daddy!" She shouted. He didn't hear her.

"Tilly-baby, come up here." Her mother picked her up, strong arms around her body. She felt her mother take two steps forward, faltering on the third.

A woman soldier with hair as smooth and short as Hankarry's from B-class stepped up, chest to chest with a grizzled old purist, not backing down.

"I'm as human as you are!"

"Franken-ware witch! Coming back stealin' all our jobs, spyin' with your wired-up eyes! Go back home!"

"This ribbon says I bled for you. I am home!" She slapped at her chest, on the left side where the iTeegs permanently displayed a purple ribbon.

"LIES! Government plants!"

The soldiers formed up and shouldered through, ignoring aggressive holographs. They circled and pushed out, forcing the purists back as the sun disappeared over the horizon line. Dantilly and her mother broke into the ring, along with a few others.

A smile bloomed on the soldier's face when he saw his wife and daughter. They slammed together in a hard hug that took Dantilly's breath away. She couldn't have been happier than in that moment.

"I'm home," he said simply. "I'm finally home."

Derek Maurer

Derek Maurer of Iowa City is a co-concierge of the Parchment Lounge. He had an unremarkable career in journalism, writing and editing for hire, PR, and marketing, but gave it all up for his sanity. Now he's writing a novel. Which is a very sane endeavor. In addition to his writing, he volunteers at the Iowa City Free Medical Clinic and gives sailing lessons at Lake Macbride as a member of the University of Iowa Sailing Club. He and his wife Linda enjoy music, camping, hiking, and easy bike trails.

The Caper

Derek Maurer

Eli saw them coming. He was standing in the corner with enough of a view out the window to observe their rapid approach to the Old Low Town Tap. There were two of them, both dressed like warehousemen, both big and physically imposing. They charged into the tavern and Eli slipped out in their wake, even before any panic erupted. He didn't know and didn't care why they had come; goons are always breaking into the places low-borns gather, he thought. His policy was, get away and stay away when they show up.

He went up to the Royal Road to be around people, then made his way toward home. Off the Royal Road the streets were dark and quiet. The eaves of the tumble-down houses cut ragged silhouettes against the moonlit sky, the never-repaired holes in the pavement beckoned passersby, and the smell of cooking fires lingered in the air. Eli took the alley behind the flat and crept through the backyard, coming in the back door so as not to disturb his ma, who surely was sleeping in the front room.

"Quiet," his sister Flor said when he let a boot drop too loudly.

"Hush yourself," Eli whispered.

Flor turned over in her pallet with a huff. Eli laid down, pulled the blanket over himself, and thought.

***

"It'll work," Eli said the next day, "we just just need to scope it and put the elements together."

Toby looked skeptical. "These guys—where were they from?"

"I don't know, upriver one way or the other," Eli said. "I think they're with different caravans. They just met, and the one was bragging about it."

"Bragging," Toby said. "About a caper. In a crowded tavern."

"So he's stupid—"

"Or a liar," Toby interjected.

"The concept was solid. We'd need a lifter and a crier, and pick the right fat duck to poach."

The two walked in silence for a while. They had passed the shit pits, which stank to high heaven in the still morning air, and the toll-takers' hut, where a line of wagons and carts bound downriver had formed, and now the canyon walls towered above them. The sound of the falls grew to a gentle roar as they rounded the bend and the valley floor fell away on their right. Here the Royal Road perched on a wide ledge carved into the rocky face. As they walked on, the falls came into view, the lower valley opened up before them, and presently they could see a line of carters far below, making their way toward the switchback.

"We'd better get down there," Toby said, and the two hurried along.

They spent the day at the switchback, pushing

carts and wagons up the steep grade for handouts and a few coins. Sometimes they worked together and sometimes apart, seeing each other only in passing. There was a good deal of traffic on the road: trading caravans coming up from Port City with goods from the coast and over the sea, and those from the interior laden with wood and copper, iron and ivory, grain and textiles and many other things, all bound for Port City. There were small bands of travelers whom you would hardly call caravans; a large group of pilgrims in their white cowls, probably headed for the shrine at Rerúam; and some wayward souls who somehow had missed the information that wayward souls generally kept to the Brown Road along the other side of the river.

About late afternoon, though hot, tired, and sore, Eli was hurrying down for another run. Just above the switchback, he overtook a skinny guy struggling to keep a rickety, overloaded handcart from running away down the hill. "Let me help you," Eli said, not even thinking to be paid for the favor. "Bloody snot!" he exclaimed somewhat involuntarily when he took hold of the harness strap and felt the weight of the load. "You're moving this by yourself?"

"I've come all the way from Ranghat," the man said. Further conversation revealed he was going to Port City to find work. He had skills in masonry and plastering, he said.

"There's no work for you in Ranghat?" Eli asked.

"Only day labor," the man said. Then he added, self-consciously, "I can't feed my family."

The next time Eli saw Toby, Toby said he was going back to town. "I'm going to work some more," Eli said. He helped push two more loads up the hill, throwing his small frame against the backs of the wagons. At least this guy's pony will be fresh for its grand entrance into the city, he thought at one point. By the time night fell and traffic had nearly ceased, he knew every rut, bump, and pothole in that section of road. His back ached and his feet were pounded raw. He made the long walk home to Low Town, past the falls glowing white in the dark depths of the canyon, past the toll takers who barely looked up from their game of sticks, past the shit pits, to where the buildings of Deeshabhat began to line the right side of the Royal Road and cultivated fields spread themselves along the river to his left. Lanterns lit the windows of apartments above the shops, and inns exhaled the smells of food cooking and of beer, tobacco, and ganja. The street echoed with the sounds of people talking and laughing and arguing and of mugs and plates meeting tables—all that life inside all those walls and here I am, thought Eli, passing by like a stranger.

***

Days passed, becoming weeks. Eli ended up at the switchback as often as not. On better days there was work to be had—hauling, digging, loading and unloading wagons at the warehouses, and many other tasks. One morning, Eli and Toby arrived at the haulers and loaders hub just as the barker called out one more open slot. "You take it," Toby said. "I'll go help my brother move his things today."

The day boss sent Eli and four others—two men and two women—to fetch wheelbarrows and haul sand, gravel, and river rocks up to a no-name intersection on High Avenue where a municipal crew was repairing the water main. The material came from the quarry where Blue Creek joined the river, down by the shit pits. When Eli's team arrived for their first load, he saw there was a gang digging out one of the old pits. Poor weasels, Eli thought, with the bad luck to be hauled in for servitude just as a shit pit needs to be dug out. Upon further reflection, he supposed it would be no coincidence if more people were rounded up when there was a big, ugly, awful job to be done.

The team stayed together, inasmuch as there were certain proportions of sand, gravel, and rock needed for the job. Plus, the team decided it would be best to trade off so that everyone shared in hauling each type of material. Eli didn't think it mattered. He couldn't tell that rock was any lighter or heavier than sand, or that sand was any easier or harder to balance than gravel. But if the other folks thought it was fair to trade off, he wasn't going to quibble. He thought it more important to get a wheelbarrow that was in good working order, and he had made sure his had a good wheel. The right handle had been repaired, though, and the rough spot was just where he had to hold it. Since he didn't have gloves, he'd have to wear blisters on that hand for a few days.

It wasn't far from the gravel yard to the job but it was uphill all the way. The loads were heavy, and if Eli got stopped it was hard to get started again. Eli's companions dumped loads in the street more than a couple times, and he was feeling superior until he dumped one himself. Ten trips made one long day with just a short break for lunch; Eli had an orange his ma made him take, though it seemed to be the last one in the flat. After the last trip, Eli and the others made west on Embral Street toward the haulers yard to return the wheelbarrows and collect their pay. A block over, at the next intersection, one of the women asked everyone to hold up a minute while she had private words with someone she knew. The others chatted and gossiped, to which Eli paid half a mind. With the other half he noted a man who stopped at a corner shop to ask the merchant about farlow root. No, said the merchant, he didn't have any. But come back next week, he told the guy, he'd have some by then.

Eli could hardly wait to tell Toby.

***

"You want to rob a place in broad daylight under the guy's nose?" Toby said.

"You're not listening," Eli replied. "You're not looking at the whole picture. The guy's not there, he gets dis-tract-ed."

"And leaves his shop unattended..."

"He's just going to be gone for a minute, is what he thinks."

"...Full of high-priced, easily fenced narcotics," Toby continued.

"You're not listening," Eli said.

The two approached the North Fork crossing cobbled together from planks and stones. Eli stepped onto the first plank and skipped lightly across that span to the next, which was set at an angle and half submerged. He continued deftly on and was standing on the far bank as Toby carefully picked his way from stone to stone across the channel.

"It's one thing to sneak into a construction yard at night and pitch stuff over the fence..." Toby said when he had reached dry ground and they'd walked a ways toward Low Town.

"You know we can sell farlow root," Eli said, "and we'll get good money for it." And after a pause: "A lot better than beat-up shovels or leavings from a caravan camp. A lot."

Toby sighed.

"Just help me scope it," Eli said. "We don't know anything till we see what the guy's deal is." They turned down Riketti Street, the low, decrepit houses crowding in from either side. Eli lowered his voice. "Come by the corner up there late in the afternoon tomorrow. Act like you've been looking for me."

They came to the street where Eli lived. "Well, so long," Eli said, and with no better offer forthcoming, he turned toward the flat. "Hey, wait a second," he said. He came close again and whispered. "Think you could ask Freddy if he wants a lifting job?" he said.

"When I see him," Toby said.

"You might have to go find him," Eli said.

"I'll ask him when I see him," Toby said. "If I can."

***

Another day, another scramble. Toby didn't show at the morning rendezvous, so Eli headed into Deeshabhat by himself. The line at the haulers and loaders hub was already too long, and as usual, the road and field work hubs were already closed. He really didn't feel like going out to the switchback, so he went over and nosed around one of the construction yards. "No, we don't have any day work today," the foreman said, not unkindly. Eli persisted, asking one of the workers if there was anything he could do for a few coins.

"Kill the foreman," the man said, flashing a grin full of rotten teeth.

Visits to a warehouse and a street repair site were no more fruitful. He decided to go hang around Commerce Street, where he had sometimes picked up coins carrying, loading, even running errands. One time, a staller who wore a ruby ring paid Eli up front to deliver a small box to his lady love. It was a very fine small box, inlaid with silver and jet. Eli crept self-consciously through the streets of High Town to the house the man had indicated. There, the maid would not let him speak to the young lady, nor even enter, but her eyes bugged out to see the box.

"That box was stolen from this house!" the maid said. "Go!"

With that, she snatched it from his hand and shut the door in his face. Eli went back to tell the staller what had happened, but the stall was closed and locked. He had not seen the man since and someone else had taken over the location.

The stallers were laying out their displays on tables and carpets when Eli got there. The only thing in short supply was customers. Eli found a shady spot and leaned his back against the wall, one foot propped up on its rough stones. He drummed his fingers on his thigh, fidgeted with the frayed hem of his shirt, and fished for the remains of a cigarette he'd found and put in his pocket. He was considering whether to go and beg a match when he heard his name.

"Eli!" said the tall, lanky, awkward figure.

"Hey Pashi," Eli said, "what are you about?"

"I'm on my way to buy pencils," Pashi said, taking his place beside Eli against the wall, leaning back and propping one foot up.

"Where do you get those?" Eli asked.

"Mr. Leo is our preferred vendor," Pashi said with an air of authority. Eli waved his hand at a fly near his face.

"How many pencils you gonna buy?" he asked.

"As many as Mr. Leo will give me for these," Pashi replied, and he opened his hand to show Eli two half-scepter coins. Pashi looked at Eli as if he were disclosing a great secret.

"That's a lot of pencils you're holding in your hand," Eli said.

"No, I haven't bought them yet!"

"No, I mean you can buy a lot of pencils with that money."

"Father says we have too many people who only use pencils," Pashi said.

The two passed the next few minutes quietly as business picked up on Commerce Street. People began poking through the piles of textiles, yarn, clothing, hats, shoes and boots, purses and wallets, woven baskets, tables and chairs, shelves, lanterns, candles, rugs, pots and pans, spoons and spatulas, bangles and baubles, flutes, tambourines, ukuleles, and many other things. Haggling and conversation rose to a low cacophony and the morning sun began to cast deep shadows under the faded awnings.

"Think you better go buy your pencils?" Eli said at last.

"Yeah," Pashi said.

"See you 'round," Eli said.

"See you square," Pashi said, grinning. He ambled off, and but for his green felt cap he would soon have been lost in the crowd.

Eli began busking, asking stallers if they needed an errand run and offering to help buyers carry their goods. He picked up a few coins that way, and so he passed the morning.

***

"Where've you been," Eli said loudly enough to be overheard.

"Where've I been," Toby ad-libbed, "I've been looking for you!"

"I'm right where I told you," Eli said.

"You said you'd wait on Hodam Street," Toby said.

"No, I said I'd be here."

"I'm pretty sure you said Hodam."

"Bloody snot!"

They walked and talked their way down Kettle Street and out of Merchant Guy's earshot. A shoemaker carried on a lively conversation with someone in his workshop; a smith plunged glowing iron into a tub of water, loosing a brief hiss and an acrid puff of steam; a small child trailed her mother up the street, crying for something they'd already passed. Toby said little except to signify he was listening as Eli described Merchant Guy's demeanor and the goings-on at his shop. "He's a hen, a ring-kisser. Which is perfect. And he gave me the once-over like four times, which is also good." Eli recounted his impressions of the customers, the

55

traffic outside the shop, Merchant Guy's attentiveness to the local environment, and other matters. At one point he confided, "He's high-end. I'll bet the lords and ladies come to him for their aphrodisiacs and 'nerve medicine'." Then, more relevantly, "He doesn't get that many people stopping in. He'll go a stretch sitting under his awning, looking bored. When somebody comes, he jumps up all smiles like he's Mister Bells-on-His-Toes."

Toby stopped and looked at Eli.

"We've gotta be able to bail on this," he said.

"Well, yeah..." Eli said.

"Even up to the last second."

"Yeah, well..." Eli stammered. "You always leave yourself a way out."

It was a couple of days before Eli returned to scope the scene some more. He came up from Hodam Square, sighting along the road to landmarks at Merchant Guy's intersection. He figured out where he could stand to watch the shop and be seen from the square a block away. He considered the different approaches and getaways. He observed the comings and goings not just in Merchant Guy's shop, but in the shops around as well. He took note of the one line of sight offering a good view into Merchant Guy's place. And he made sure Merchant Guy saw him again.

When Toby came, he brought bad news. "Freddy won't do it," he said.

"Why not?" Eli said.

"Ghosts," Toby said. Apparently ghosts told Freddie he had shadows attached to his spine, and the bad things he did made the shadows stronger. Freddie seemed to have become obsessed with the shadows' tightening grip on him.

"Ghosts," Eli pondered.

"I asked him who we could get," Toby said. "He didn't want to say because of the shadows. But I finally got a name out of him: his cousin Sneel."

"Sneel's a puke," Eli said.

***

"Like I said, he's a weasel," Eli told Toby. "I'd like to find someone who's not so weaselly."

"Well, let me just tap into my vast network of contacts in the criminal underworld," Toby said. They walked quickly away from the Old Low Town Tap and turned a corner because, Eli said, he didn't want Sneel to see which way they went. Up Broad Street with its shuttered shops, down Standin, and up Cutoff toward Five Corners until Eli was satisfied they were well clear of any hint of Sneel.

"I think I heard him say he'd do it," Toby said.

Eli sighed and said, "But he is a weasel. And he looks like a rat with those whiskers."

"We all have our faults." Eli rolled his eyes. Toby continued, "You didn't tell him about Pashi..."

"Pashi's none of his business," Eli said. They stood now at Five Corners, where the sparse foot traffic was mostly men going home from the taverns. Eli's flat was that-away and Toby's place the other way. There was no moon, so starlight and a few lanterns were all there was to see by. A small group of drunks sloshed past, arguing about a missed call in the afternoon ball game and then breaking into song when they got further up the street. A black and white cat hurried along carrying a limp mouse in its mouth.

"So you don't think the lifter needs to know we have an imbecile working the caper..."

"He's not an imbecile!" Eli said defiantly. "And it's because he's simple that this works perfectly. And who his father is. He's above suspicion." Suddenly aware his voice might be carrying, he lowered it to a whisper. "Pashi's got more decency in his nose than Weasel does in his whole ugly face." Neither spoke again for a long moment.

"Look," Eli said, "he'll think it's a game. He gets to hang out with us and he gets to keep a secret. He can do it."

The next day, or the day after, Eli was back up at Merchant Guy's intersection. He stationed himself where he could see into the shop and scoped what he could of its interior. Mostly there were shelves and shelves of bottles and jars, filled with liquids and powders and pastes. There were bins and baskets of loose leaves, roots, bark, and the like. Eli could see that the inventory was neatly labeled and he wondered if Sneel could read. There was a counter with two scales on it, a large one and a small one. Eli watched inconspicuously as Merchant Guy served a customer, taking a jar from the shelf, placing weights on one end of the small scale and spooning powder from the jar into the other pan. When he had ostentatiously demonstrated that the powder weighed a li-i-ittle more than even on the scale, Merchant Guy carefully scraped the powder into a paper envelope and handed it over to the customer. The woman, who looked like a house maid, pulled out a purse that hung around her neck and paid Merchant Guy with silver coins.

The woman left and Merchant Guy disappeared through a door in the back corner of the shop. When he returned a few minutes later, he found a man with a package waiting outside.

"Come in, come in!" Merchant Guy said.

Eli couldn't hear their conversation, but he watched as Merchant Guy opened the package, wrapped in muslin and tied with string. It revealed a wooden box big enough for a pair of shoes. Merchant Guy lifted the lid and leaned over to sniff the contents, his eyes closing and his nose wrinkling before a broad smile spread across his face. Back he went to the back room, emerging moments later with his own purse. The coins he handed the man were definitely gold and not brass.

When Toby came by, Eli was emphatic. "We've gotta move on this," he said.

***

Eli stood against the corner of the building, his posture a study in nonchalance, his eyes a study in active surveillance. The streets were busy but not overcrowded. Across the intersection, Sneel loitered as inconspicuously as he knew how, which is to say, not very. Down the street at Hodam Square, Toby was coaching Pashi, holding him back, reminding him what to do. Everybody knew the signal: Eli would reach up with his right hand and scratch his head. Standing on one leg, his other foot propped against the wall, Eli drummed his fingers on his thigh lightly, almost imperceptibly, and waited. Toby waved to get Eli's attention. He pointed to a woman in blue who was making her way up the street.

Dame Lobelia, tall and elegant in her long embroidered day gown and matching wide-brimmed hat, nodded ever-so-slightly to Merchant Guy as she passed his shop. Her noble bearing was accentuated by the attendant who followed close behind, a young man in a uniform who carried several packages and affected an air of self-importance. Merchant Guy answered her nod with a deferent bow of his head as she continued up the street trailing a whiff of perfume. Perfect, Eli thought.

Just then, as it happened, a bee following the perfume that wafted Eli's way grazed his hair and hovered near his face. Startled, he waved at it with his hand and tried to jump clear. A block away, Pashi was off like a terrier. By the time Eli saw Pashi galloping up the street, he barely had the chance to catch Sneel's eye. Well, he thought, the caper's on. He pulled himself around the corner and out of sight so as not to distract Pashi, who was approaching fast and beginning to call out his line.

"Dame Lobelia!" Pashi yelled. "You forgot your package!"

Eli wished Dame Lobelia was further away—he could still see her hat gliding gracefully up the next block.

"Dame Lobelia, you forgot your package!" Pashi called again as he passed Merchant Guy's shop. At this rate Pashi would soon be upon Dame Lobelia, and Eli hoped he would remember there was no package and he was not really supposed to catch her. No matter. The thing now was how Merchant Guy would respond. He nibbled at the bait, rising from his bench to come look up the street to where Pashi still chased Dame Lobelia. Then Pashi caught up to her, and she and her attendant and Pashi all stood in plain sight at the end of the next block. Eli imagined her trying to explain to Pashi she had done no such thing as leave a package behind. With only the barest hint of reluctance to leave his shop, Merchant Guy broke into a trot toward the lady in distress, no doubt to offer his help in resolving her difficulty.

Eli nodded at Sneel, who slipped into Merchant Guy's shop and began looking for jars of powdered farlow root. Eli's heart was pounding. He looked up the street to see that Dame Lobelia appeared now to be lecturing Pashi, while Sneel scanned the bins and shelves. Merchant Guy seemed to have tired and was now just waddling up the street. Sneel eased his way to the back corner of the shop and the door that led to the back room. He looked at Eli across the street corner. Eli glanced up the street, then back at Sneel, signaling him to hurry up. Sneel lifted the door's latch and carefully pulled it open. Then all hell broke loose.

A dog that had been sleeping inside the back room started barking, scrambled to its feet, and lunged at Sneel. Sneel fell back and knocked over some jars and baskets, which crashed to the floor, breaking glass and spreading powder and dried herbs everywhere. Merchant Guy heard his dog barking, turned, and came running with surprising speed and agility. And worst of all, two guys appeared from nowhere and converged on the shop. "Goons!" Eli said under his breath as he watched in horror the caper's unravelling. Between the dog and the broken glass, Sneel struggled to get away from the shop, but it was too late. The goons had him. He fought and kicked, but they had him. Panicked, he looked Eli's way and tried to point.

"There! Him!" Sneel shouted. "His name's Eli. It's his caper!"

Eli had already turned and begun running.

***

Down Kettle Street, past Line Street to where Kettle met Hodam and angled toward the Royal Road. Through the small market and up the Royal Road past the long row of shops, warehouses, and inns on one side and the citrus orchard on the other, Eli sprinted and didn't look back. He had no plan of where to go. Finally it occurred to him that running flat out was a good way to get noticed. He slowed to a brisk walk, gasping and exhausted, and entered Confluence Market, where it was crowded, noisy, and hot. As far as he knew he had shaken his pursuer, if there even was one. He did what he could to blend into the crowd amid the stalls. His thoughts were a riot, and the blistering sun cast everything in silhouette. The sounds of people talking and of a beggar's violin seemed distant, from another world. The smells of onions and meat cooking on grills, and of sweat and piss, were sickening.

Feeling more at ease after a short spell in the crowded market, Eli ambled for a time among the sellers as if he were shopping for pomegranates or a child's toy. But he turned quickly away when he noticed someone he recognized ahead. He left the market and walked up Werrin Street, where brokers and traders had their shop fronts. Now he felt exposed and looked all around. A pair of windows felt to him like spying eyes. People's glances looked suspicious. Snatches of conversation that he overheard all featured words that sounded like "Eli" and "Bounty". How long had it been since the caper, he wondered. If the goons put bounty shares out on him, how fast could word spread? He needed to get home and warn his ma that goons were after him. He needed to find someplace where he could think and plan his next move. Then he remembered: the rendezvous! He was supposed to meet Toby at Mane's tavern after the caper, when they thought they would have farlow powder to sell. What a relief it would be to see Toby, he thought. They could put their heads together and figure out what to do.

He began to take his bearings and calculate the risks of every route out of there. Any way to get to Mane's seemed rife with traps. He could avoid the day labor hubs, but if he went through the warehouse district he might see cargadores who knew him; if he took to the markets and the main streets it could be anybody; and if he took a long way around through neighborhoods he'd stand out like a tall weed in the oats. He couldn't move and he dare not stay. The least bad option, he decided, was to work his way around the markets and warehouses on the comparatively quiet streets of the Limestone District. If someone gave chase to him there, he would see it coming and could try to flee.

He had just one real fright along the way. A bunch of kids came running into the street behind him chasing a ball and Eli nearly panicked, breaking into a sprint before realizing there was no threat. Otherwise, his uneventful passage along the narrow streets, with their smooth paving stones, gave him a chance to rage internally against anyone who would betray a brother for a bounty share. The low-born should stick together, he seethed. First the rich control every penny we can earn, then they turn us against each other so none of us ever gets ahead. I have never, I would never put the dart on one of our own, he thought, not for petty theft. Stealing from each other is a crime, rape and murder are crimes, but stealing from the rich when you're hungry is just getting by.

Then he started to think through what had happened—how had the caper gone bad? There was the obvious miscue that sent Pashi running too soon, and the dog was a nasty surprise. But what Eli couldn't fathom was how quickly the goons had appeared. How likely was it that they just happened to be nearby and heard the racket? He didn't see them until they were practically upon Sneel; they seemed to come from nowhere. Were they tipped off and ready? No one but Sneel could have done that, and if he did, then he was a better actor than thief, the biting and scratching and kicking he did...

This was Eli's train of thought as he neared Mane's. He had to take to Section Avenue for half a block to get there, and he was wary and alert. He looked up and down the street before crossing into the tavern's doorway, where he stood half in and half out to scan the room. No Toby. It looked like a bunch of regulars having coffee or beer. He went in and sat at a table by the wall, where he could see out the window without being seen, and asked for tea when Mane's wife came for his order. Toby should have been there already, Eli thought. He wasn't even sure what Toby could have known about the fracas—he was a block away from the scene. Did he see the scuffle? Did he see Eli break and run? Did he try to find out what happened? Did Sneel put the dart on him, too? Did Toby get nabbed for bounty?

And what if he did get nabbed, Eli wondered. Would he turn on me to save himself?

Or maybe Toby had already been to Mane's and left when Eli didn't show up. With no way to know, Eli sat as if under a spell, his fingers drumming the table lightly and his leg bouncing beneath it. Then he realized he had to get out of there. His patience gone, he decided to take the low-water crossing to Low Town. He had to tell his ma what was up, and she might be able to help him. He got up, paid for the tea with some of his last coins, and went out into the late afternoon. He didn't look around now, he just turned toward the river, crossed the Royal Road, and descended along the avenue's path through the farm plots. The crossing came into view and there were a couple of women and some kids on the opposite bank washing clothes. Eli heard footsteps behind him, someone with a heavy footfall walking quickly or running slowly. He wheeled around to see Bermel, a man he knew from day labor, trotting toward him, out of breath.

"Eli!" Bermel called. "Eli, wait."

Eli tensed himself, ready to fight or flee, as Bermel came near. "Eli, they're after you," Bermel huffed. "Some goons put bounty shares out on you."

"What for?" Eli said. "I've just been working."

"I don't know what for," Bermel said. "I just know word's getting around. Be careful." Bermel stood a little too close, and Eli backed away.

"Yeah, I'll be careful," he said.

Bermel stood panting and didn't speak for a moment. Then he lunged at Eli and managed to grab him. Eli's arm was free and he smacked Bermel in the face. The two struggled. Bermel was bigger but he was no match for Eli's energy. Eli kicked and elbowed the older man and stomped on his foot, and soon broke free. It happened that his momentum carried him back toward the Royal Road, and he ran for all he was worth. He had no thoughts at all, he just ran, and when he came to the Royal Road he turned toward the Confluence.

He flew and did not look left or right, through the crowded plaza where the Royal Road branched, where the constabulary and the toll-takers and tax-collectors had their stations. Agile, unbound by ordinary limitations, he aimed himself at the lane down into the cultivated fields along the river, and in he glided. Past the plots of grain and vegetables, past the stand of olive trees, past where old Dorey had taught him how to weed and tend, he ran, still guided by some process that did not involve his conscious thought. He turned into a path between farm plots and slowed to a trot as he made his way toward the river. He left the fields and crashed into the willows, exhaustion catching up to him. And when he could see nothing but green leaves and river grasses and swaying branches, he collapsed.

***

Eli lay in a little depression looking up through leaves and branches stirred by the river breeze. The afternoon sun was beginning to sink toward evening and the swishing leaves let shafts of light fall across his eyes. Wispy clouds blew noiselessly across his field of view, visible against the blue sky through shifting openings in the low canopy. Softly rustling leaves and the gentle voice of the nearby river were the only sounds that met his ears. The smells of mud and rotting fish filled his nose. A bug of some sort, probably an ant, crawled across his neck and under his shirt, and he became absorbed for a time in that sensation, a light tickle that was not in itself objectionable.

For a short while, Eli's predicament seemed far away. The sunlight through the leaves, the murmuring waters, and the feel of the breeze above were enough to calm him. When his thoughts wandered, they drifted toward those days not so many years ago when he was still growing and worked for Dorey, a skinny, white-haired woman with a nasty cough, weeding and tending her garden plot. That would have been this time of year, he thought. It was just over there, not far from this spot. He didn't know anything about gardening. She said she picked him out of the line because he was small and couldn't do much harm. She put him to work among the carrots and beets and onions and taught him how to pull up weeds.

"Don't tear at them," she scolded. Then, softening, "Get them out by the roots as much as you can." She made sure he could tell the difference between the weeds and the crops; he looked across the field and saw only weeds, they having a good head start. She made him work by hand, though she herself used a hoe, puffing on the pipe clenched between her teeth. She gave him a broad-brimmed hat that was too big for his head. Dorey would leave him alone for hours, but came to check up on him and bring him lemon water. Then she started bringing him fruit and lentil cakes. Slowly the weeds disappeared and the rows of crops took form. Dorey came along where he had weeded and thinned the plants, unsentimentally pulling up half of those Eli had painstakingly preserved. They used the pulled-up weeds and plants to mulch between the rows.

At the end of each day she handed him a half-scepter coin and told him to come back tomorrow. As far as he was concerned, he'd found the honey pot: steady work for food and money besides. Then one day, the couple who had come around from time to time to talk and argue with Dorey were there to greet him first thing. "We don't need you today," the guy said.

"Where's Dorey?" Eli asked.

"She's sick," the woman said.

"When should I come back?" Eli asked.

"We don't need you to come back," the guy said.

There didn't seem to be any more he could say or do, so Eli went away. He never saw Dorey again. A couple of times, he ventured down the lane past her plot and saw other people working it.

Now the ants were getting to Eli. He jumped up and shook his legs, and took off his shirt and shook it out. There was still plenty of daylight left, though, and he wanted to wait till dark to make for home. He began to fret over how he would get there. If he'd had half a brain, he thought, he'd have run the other way from his scuffle with Bermel and would already be in Low Town. Now he'd have to cross the river, and it was either get wet—really wet—or take to one of the roads. And what had happened to Toby? They were partners, and more than partners. To think Toby could either desert or betray him was beyond Eli's imagining. His thoughts cycled through the possibilities: Toby didn't see what happened, and he went to Mane's and waited, and when Eli didn't show, he left. Or, Toby saw the commotion and was too scared to go to Mane's. Or, Ratface (Eli's newest name for Sneel) put the dart on Toby, and he'd either been nabbed or was hiding out himself. Or... Toby was the rat.

Eli shrank from that last thought as if from a withering flame.

It couldn't be. Or, it was the only explanation. The very question made Eli swoon.

A couple of hours passed. The sun disappeared behind the bluff and the first-quarter moon began to sink toward the horizon. Eli crept from his little thicket of river willows to a place where he could watch Palace Road. It was too late now for field work and the last of the farm laborers made their ways to wherever they were going. When the part of the road he could see had been deserted for several minutes, Eli edged closer and looked both ways, up toward town and out toward the bridge. He saw no one. He stood and mounted the road, briskly walking the short stretch to the bridge. Still no one. As much as he wanted to seem nonchalant—nobody here but us laborers going home after a long day in the fields—he couldn't stop himself from running when he reached the top of the bridge's high arch. When he got to the far side he pitched himself into a squash patch and scrambled on his hands and knees to the willows along the river. His hands and arms were dirty and itched like crazy from brushing against the leaves and vines, sweat ran into his eyes and made them sting, and his chest heaved as he gasped for breath. He lay on the damp ground under the willows for a good while, resting and collecting his thoughts. One more crossing to go.

He got up and stumbled through the willows, tripping on rocks and roots and knocking into branches, making his way upstream toward the bridge between Low Town and the palace. Soon he found himself among the cottonwoods, the understory clearer and easier to walk through. Then he began to see the effigies hanging from branches, hundreds of them throughout the grove, ghostly, glowing ghastly in the moonlight. He discerned a path and followed it. He heard people shuffling along Palace Road and it gave him some confidence he could take the bridge without drawing attention to himself, for it was not too late to be out. But his confidence faltered as he got to where he could see the palace gates. It seemed there were a lot of uniformed guards and people about. He couldn't get to the bridge without mounting the road and passing in full view.

Eli backed slowly away from his vantage point, plunking his foot into a mud puddle and causing a splash he thought must have resounded through the valley. He held perfectly still and listened intently for any sound of pursuit. Hearing none, he made his way back into the grove. He knew what he had to do. He must ford the South Fork to get to Low Town.

***

Eli drummed his fingers lightly on the dirty glass pane but didn't dare show himself at the back window. A long moment passed and he drummed again, this time a little louder. Finally he heard floorboards creaking inside, and the door latch lifted slowly and quietly. "Eli!" his ma whispered. "Get inside and be quiet!"

She seemed to be alone, no sign of his sister. Eli could see through to the front room of the flat, where a single candle burned. "It's not safe here," his ma said, still whispering. "The goons have been here looking for you."

"I know, Ma," Eli replied. "I gotta get away for awhile."

"What happened, Eli? What have you done?"

"Caper went bad. A rat-faced puke put the dart on me." The two looked at each other, his ma's graying hair backlit from the other room. It was the first time Eli had ever spoken to her about his grifting.

"Where will you go?" she asked.

"Down to the coast, to Port City. I can get work there."

She sniffled, and Eli saw tears streaming down her cheeks. After a long pause, holding her bowed head in her hand, she said, "I don't want you to go, Eli, I want to know where you are."

"I'll be in servitude if I stay!" he whispered fiercely.

"We'll buy you out, we'll get the money somehow." Now she was weeping. "If you turn yourself in, I'll know where you are, and we can get money and buy you out."

Eli had dreaded a painful, unbearable parting. He listened helplessly as his ma pleaded again for him to turn himself into the authorities. She was on a roll. She had already figured he could go straight to the magistracy and at least cut the goons out of their bounty. Dogs barked nearby, startling them.

"Ma, I can't stay," Eli said when quiet returned. "I can't go in servitude." She didn't argue anymore. He went to the corner where he kept his belongings and changed into his work boots as his ma stifled her sobs. He put his empty bota over his shoulder and then pulled on his poncho and hat. "Here's some money. I've got a little more to get me to Port City." He took her hand and put a few battered coins in it and then, tenderly, closed her fingers around them.

"Oh, Eli," she said, "when will I see you again?"

"I don't know. I'll come back when I can. I'll get lots of money so you can buy a house and we'll live like lords and ladies." She broke down crying again. Someone knocked something over in the street and the dogs renewed their barking. Eli's heart practically jumped from his chest. Instinctively he withdrew into the shadows and out of sight from the front window. The woman upstairs yelled down to the street and the guy in the street yelled back, and Eli couldn't wait to get out of there.

"I've gotta go, Ma," he said. They embraced, both of them crying. "I'll come back when I can, when the dart's off me."

"Don't get mixed up in things," his ma said. "Stay clear of all that."

Only when he had crept through the willows, forded the river, and scrambled to the heights above the valley did Eli begin to relax. By dawn, when he had found his way down to the Brown Road in the lower valley, he began to see the way ahead and not behind. Work will be easier to get in Port City, he thought, and I'll save some money. Maybe I'll bring Ma and Flor down there. Forget about Deeshabhat.

It's no place for a queer boy, anyway.

Alexandra Penn

Alexandra Penn was a museum kid. The daughter of a photographer and a Scuba diver, she spent her teenage years in the field: Penn has worked with Smithsonian archaeologists, NASA software engineers, volcanologists, and photographers. She also managed to fail Algebra II with a passing grade, which she's a little proud of.

Her work is both a love letter to and an intense criticism of the academic world.

She has been bitten by a shark, she watched the final shuttle launch from the fire escape outside Launch Control, and she has been a certified diver since age twelve. She likes dogs, long walks on the beach, and socialized medicine. Also books.

Penn is one of two Directors of The Writers' Rooms (you may know her from the cover as Alex Penland), an editor for hire, an amateur linguist, and a Taurus. Her work has received many accolades, including an Honorable Mention in the Writer's Digest Annual Contest 2017.

You can buy her serial, *The Letter Mage*, on

Amazon—and be sure to leave a review!

She spends all her free time on Twitter. Follow her @AlexPenname.

Dear Future Soulmate no. 1

Alexandra Penn

One day, you'll learn:
I've never been one for love stories.
The last time a gorgeous man
(in Greece of all places)
on a beach, while the sun set around us
bought me a rose
I blushed, said thank you very much,
and proceeded to ignore him
for a week.
I kept the rose.
One day, you'll learn:
I'm terrible at knowing when you flirt,
because while I'm confident enough
to conquer cities
to rule planets
I am such a stereotype
and even at my healthiest
I did not think I was worthy
of love.
One day, you'll learn:
it's not that I don't want you
it's that I need you to challenge me,
prove to me that I am worth loving
prove to me that I am worth giving
up that little piece of your soul
that I can let down the walls
and disband the theater
of my fortressed heart.
One day, you'll learn:
how efficient I am at protecting

everything I desire and hold dear.
One day I hope that you will be
encompassed in that shield
shattering it from within
freeing us both
escaping the prison
of my own making.

Dear Future Soulmate no. 2

Alexandra Penn

baggage, a list for reference:
I. failed love interest (male)
contains
9 years friendship
3 sabotaged mutual acquaintances
1 family member, no longer spoken to
II. abusive partner (female)
contains
gaslighting (for duration)
bruises on the heart (contained by walls)
a dislike of mormon girls (irrational)
III. shoes to fill (female)
contains
empty space
feathers (lost from new wings)
fear of heights
IV. divorce (parental)
contains
fear of commitment (genetic)
blueprint for relationships (defective)
introspection to the point of failure (predisposed)

please refer to items when necessary.

Dear Future Soulmate no. 3

Alexandra Penn

I am writing to say
thank you.
As of this letter,
you have stood with me
through all future arguments,
through my harping
on small things
that mean we cannot possibly last,
through my projecting
all disagreements
fifty years into the future,
through the bad days at work
and rejection letters,
through the holes punched in
where old lovers failed me
and old friends left me
and fairy tales died
through the scars left by parents
who only loved visions of each other
through romance novels
you could never possibly live up to.

I am working on it
right now
so when I meet you
maybe I won't be so
broken.

Erin Casey

Erin Casey graduated from Cornell College in 2009 with degrees in English and Secondary Education. She decided to expand upon her teaching knowledge by leading writing sessions at first for the Iowa Writers' House and now for The Writers' Rooms. She attended the Denver Publishing Institute in 2009 and has been a recruiter ever since. She is the Communications and Student Relationships Manager at The Iowa Writers' House. She's also a devoted bird mom of seven. When not volunteering and working, she's writing her LGBT YA fantasy story, as well as a mix of medieval fantasy and urban fantasy books. Currently, she is publishing her debut urban fantasy book called *The Purple Door District* on December 15, 2018. To find out more and follow her on social media, visit her at www.erincasey.org.

Fathoms Below
Erin Casey

Chapter 1: Stowaway

Cassandra sat up, chains weighing heavily on her wrists. Her little prison was dark and cold, the only light coming from a single lantern rocking on a peg across from her. She frowned. The lantern was moving much too quickly.

The ship lurched.

Cassandra was thrown against the wall, but her restraints kept her from going far. Timber groaned as waves crashed against the side of the boat. Sailors' frightened shouts were drowned out by roaring thunder. She didn't understand. The sea had been calm moments ago and yet it felt like they were being swept up in a maelstrom.

Another crash of waves sent the lantern flying off of the peg. It shattered, spilling whale oil and fire across the wood. The hungry flames devoured the liquid and started to spread across the hull of the ship.

Cassandra scrambled away from it. "Help! Help!" she screamed. She doubted anyone would come for her, though.

She was just a stowaway.

The fire grew brighter and began to fill the room with smoke. She coughed and jerked as hard as she could against her manacles. It was no use. Crackling flames crawled closer and closer to her feet. She pulled her knees up to her chest and said a prayer to the sea goddess Calypso.

Suddenly, the timbers gave a death moan. Wood fractured and bent. Water gushed through the ship's mortal wound and snuffed out the fire before it started to fill the hull.

Cassandra cried out and renewed her struggles, even as the water went past her hips, her chest, and finally her head. The suction yanked her towards the gaping hole. Only the chains kept her from being thrown out to the ocean. But what good was that when she couldn't breathe?

Someone…help, she begged.

Her lungs screamed for air. She held her breath as long as she could until her lips parted and drank in the salty ocean.

Something moved out of the corner of her eye. The last thing she saw was a pale white hand reaching for her black bound wrist.

Chapter 2: The Mermaid

Cassandra woke with a gasp, water gushing out of her mouth. She rolled over and hacked up the salty liquid onto a stone floor. Her mind spun and her chest hurt like she'd been struck by something heavy.

"Thank the goddess you're alive," a soft voice said.

Cassandra jerked in alarm and looked around. The walls were made of stone, like a cave, but before her was a giant pool of water that gently lapped at her damp body. Her vision was hazy and it took her a moment to focus on the figure floating in the water. She scrubbed a hand across her eyes and blinked.

A woman smiled back at her, her blue and green hair cascading like a waterfall around her pale face. Iridescent scales sparkled in patches on her cheeks and neck. Her exposed torso bore scales across her bare breasts, while long strings of pearls and violet flowers swayed in her hair.

The woman raised her hand in a gesture of peace. At first, webbing stretched between her fingertips. But as her hand dried, her delicate fingers parted. "I mean you no harm."

"Who are you? Where am I?" Cassandra asked. She tried not to be drawn into the woman's violet eyes, but she couldn't help herself; they were so beautiful.

The woman swam closer, folding her arms on the stony ledge. "Rest. I found you in a shipwreck. You were tethered to the side of the boat and drowning. I freed you and brought you here. It's a secret grotto where you can be safe as you recover."

Cassandra blinked and looked down at her free wrists. She rubbed them, feeling the hot bruises beneath her fingertips. Not all of them were due to the manacles.

"My name is Nimue," the woman said. "Who are you?"

"C-Cassandra," she replied. "I'm...no one."

Nimue frowned deeply. "Why were you chained, and why did no one come to help you?"

"I was a stowaway," Cassandra said before hesitating. She wasn't sure how much she should say, but there was something in Nimue's eyes that said she could trust her. "I ran away from my husband and hid on a ship dressed as a boy." She gestured to her breeches and her sailor attire which were now damp and torn from her plight. "But I was discovered. They chained me below, intending to bring me back to my husband, but then..." She frowned. "What of the sailors?"

"No one survived. Well, no one except you."

"I thank you for that," Cassandra replied. She couldn't feel much sympathy for the men who had left her to die at the bottom of the vessel. She slowly calmed down and scooted closer to the woman. "How were you able to save me? Do you have a ship?"

Nimue laughed, a pretty sound that echoed in the cave. "I don't really have need of a ship." She floated backwards and lifted her legs.

No...not legs.

A tail.

Iridescent scales with a whisper of purple shimmered in the bioluminescence of the grotto. Her fin was even more beautiful with splashes of violet, blue, and green.

"A mermaid..." Cassandra breathed.

Nimue bit her lip. "You're not afraid of me, are you?"

"I didn't even know you existed!" Cassandra cried. "My mother used to tell me fairytales about mermaids and creatures of the sea, but I never thought you were real." She crawled forward like an eager child and stretched out her hand. She paused, fingers hovering. "May I?"

The mermaid grinned and floated a little closer until Cassandra felt the cool, smooth scales under her fingertips. She closed her eyes, remembering a time when she was still innocent. When her mother sang sweet lullabies and her father rocked her on his knee.

Cassandra felt Nimue staring at her, and she opened her eyes. "Beautiful."

A blush blossomed across Nimue's cheeks. "So are you."

"Why did you save me?" Cassandra asked as she pulled her hand away. "Of all the people on that ship, you rescued me."

"You're innocent," Nimue replied. "I couldn't let you go to Davy Jones' locker."

Cassandra cocked her head to the side. "But how do you know? I was chained and those sailors weren't."

"I've seen that ship before," Nimue said in a low tone. "Capturing creatures of the sea, ferrying along men, women, children, and even mermaids in chains. Why should I help the ones who torment their own people and mine?"

Cassandra couldn't argue. Bruises still lined her back, and it had nothing to do with the ship sinking. Men could be so cruel, especially the one who had professed to love her.

"Cassandra?" Nimue said. "Are you all right?"

Cassandra blinked, noticing that tears blurred her vision. She brushed them away with her sleeve. "I don't know where to go. If I return to land, my husband will find me."

Nimue tilted her head. "But, if he's your husband, doesn't that mean you love him?"

"No," Cassandra almost spat the word. "I was forced to marry him, and he is abusive, malicious, and has no respect for me. I don't love him." She gave a bitter laugh. "I don't think I've ever loved anyone."

"Neither have I," Nimue admitted. She glanced sideways at Cassandra. "You could stay here. I can bring you food and things from the shore. At least until you're healed and you know where you want to go."

"But why?" Cassandra asked. "You hardly know me!"

Nimue blushed. "Because I would like to know someone who has a kind heart. Please, let me help you."

"More than you already have?"

"Please," Nimue practically begged. "Let me do some good in this world."

Cassandra thought it a peculiar thing to say, but with nowhere else to go, she agreed.

Chapter 3: Water Dance

For the next several days, Cassandra rested in her underwater grotto. But she was not without comfort. Nimue came frequently, bringing with her furniture and treasures from sunken ships. Before long, her secret home bore a woven rug, a couch, dresses, brushes, silvers and golds. She woke one morning to find a net of sweet fruits, salted meats, and a barrel of fresh water. Cassandra enjoyed every bite, but she left enough for Nimue.

Each time Nimue stayed, they sat up for hours talking about their worlds. Cassandra told her about her village. She described its cobblestone streets, the smell of fresh bread wafting through the bakery window, and the festivals and dances she had attended over the years.

"I love to dance," Nimue said, her arms propped on the stone shore.

Cassandra lay on her belly, their elbows almost touching. "How? You don't have legs."

"We can dance in the ocean too," Nimue laughed. She held out her hand. "Let me show you."

Cassandra didn't hesitate. She threw off her gown, leaving on her undergarments, and slid into the water. Nimue took one of her hands and wrapped an arm around Cassandra's waist. She started to swim them in circles, bobbing as she went and making Cassandra giggle with giddiness.

"Hold your breath!" Nimue ordered before she pulled them both under the water.

Cassandra couldn't open her eyes, but she felt Nimue pull her closer and spin her in graceful circles. It was almost as if she was upon a dancefloor beneath the waves!

When Nimue brought her up for air, and their heads broke the surface, they both laughed, their voices echoing in the cave. Cassandra leaned into Nimue's arms for support and smiled at her. "You're a wonderful dancer."

"As are you," Nimue replied with a shy smile.

They floated together in the water, slowly circling as they held onto one another. "I've told you about myself," Cassandra said softly. "What of you?"

"I live with my mother. My father died when I was very young, and I have always felt responsible for her. We built a home in a cave filled with coral, seaweed, and treasures from ships. It's so beautiful, Cassandra. We are part of a kingdom protected by our queen, Ociana." Her eyes grew sad. "But, my mother fell ill, and so I have had to work to heal her."

Cassandra squeezed her arm sympathetically. "I lost my mother to sickness when I was but a child. My father hardened his heart to me; it was he who sold me to my husband. Will your mother live?"

Nimue forced a smile. "So long as I do as I am asked."

"What do you mean?"

The mermaid's face colored and she glanced away.

Cassandra touched her cheek. "Nimue?"

"It's nothing for you to fret over," Nimue said and brought Cassandra back to the shore. She helped Cassandra out of the water and touched her leg. "Rest." And before Cassandra could say a word, the mermaid fled into the depths.

Cassandra did not stop thinking about Nimue's words. What promise had she made? How was she keeping her mother alive? Did she need currency? The questions niggled at her.

When Nimue returned the next day, Cassandra clasped her hands. "What ails your mother? We have earth remedies, and I know a witch who may help."

But Nimue pulled away and shook her head. "I can't. I have already made an oath to save her life. Please, Cassandra, ask me no more questions about her. I can save her; I just need a little more time." She sighed and touched

Cassandra's hand. "Perhaps it is time that you return to shore where you belong."

"I don't want to go," Cassandra protested. "I want to stay here, with you."

Nimue sucked in a breath and shut her eyes tightly. A tear slipped down her cheek, splashing into the water. "You can't. It's not safe for you here."

Cassandra tensed. "What do you mean? If you're in danger—"

"There's nothing you can do for me," Nimue said. She reached up and touched Cassandra's cheek. A sad smile touched her lips. "Nothing…except stay safe."

Cassandra made to protest, but a strange sensation filled her. Blue light danced in front of her eyes, power that matched the magic filling Nimue's hand. Her eyelids grew heavy, and she collapsed.

Chapter 4: The Witch

The cry of a seagull shook Cassandra from her forced slumber. Sunlight warmed her cheeks and arms while waves tickled her fingers. She sat up with a start, finding herself at the edge of a beach.

There was no sign of Nimue.

"No…no, Nimue!" she cried.

Only the ocean and a distant ship bell answered her.

Cassandra paced the length of the shore, hands clasped in her curly hair. She didn't know where their secret grotto was or how she could get back to Nimue. If she went to town, she might be recognized. And if she hid on a ship, she could be discovered again. Even then, what would she do if she had no fins?

She paused.

She didn't have fins now, but what if someone could grant them to her?

Someone like a witch.

Cassandra ran, her feet kicking up sand and shells. There were stories of a witch who hid near the coastline. Few went to her, fearing that the wrath of their holy God would strike them down. But Cassandra couldn't just leave Nimue to face her dangers alone, whatever they might be.

The beach dipped down as cliffs rose beside her. She climbed through rocks, not caring as they cut into her feet, until she came upon an opening where water sloshed into the mountain. The entrance was dank and dark, an eerie chill coming out of the rock's gaping mouth. She looked inside, but she couldn't see anything.

"Hello?" she called. "I seek the witch!"

A voice spoke just beside her ear, causing her to jump. "No need to shout."

A crone stood before her, her straggled black and silver hair held behind her with strands of seaweed. Her dress was made of fishing nets, sea shells, scales, and hooks that jingled as she stepped towards Cassandra. The water separating them seemed to part beneath the witch's bony feet. She smiled and pointed a gnarled finger at Cassandra. "You come seeking a spell."

"Y-yes," Cassandra said nervously. She looked the woman up and down and flinched as a purple crab crawled through the witch's hair and settled upon her shoulder like an old friend. "I wish to give up my legs for fins."

"Ah, another lovesick fool," the witch scoffed. "When will you learn that humans should stay on land, and sea beasts should remain there?" She wagged her finger at the golden ring on Cassandra's finger. "Get you back to your husband. The sea is not for you. Your heart has already been claimed."

"He will never have my heart," Cassandra growled. She ripped the ring from her finger. "It belongs to another."

The witch's eyes glinted greedily as she stared at the ring. "The ocean is not as kind as it once was, girl. More than one ship has gone to Davy Jones; his magic fills these waves. No matter what spell I give you, I cannot promise that it will do as you hope."

"I. Don't. Care." Cassandra thrust the ring at her. "Take this as payment. Please. My...friend's life may be in danger."

The witch snatched the ring of bondage away and bit the tip. Her lips pulled up into a wide smile. She handed it to the crab who took the ring in his big claw. "Very well. Stand there." She pointed at the water.

Cassandra stepped into it and faced the witch. Her heart pounded in her chest. Was this truly what she wanted? She might never return to the shore again.

But what was left for her on land?

Nimue's face formed in her mind, and the mermaid's sweet laugh filled her ears. Cassandra couldn't let her go.

The witch pulled a small bottle out from beneath her netted dress and poured it into the water. Golden magic rushed towards Cassandra and started to crawl up her legs. Her flesh tingled and her toes started to ache.

"What's happening?" she cried.

"Exactly what you asked for," the witch said.

The magic climbed higher and higher until it covered Cassandra from the waist down. She threw her head back and cried out in pain as her legs cracked and melded together. She lost her footing and fell into the water. And still the pain did not stop. Her clothing and flesh fell away as scales took form, fighting the cold of the ocean.

Soon, the magic faded.

Cassandra winced and leaned back. She had to concentrate to pull her legs, no, her tail, out of the water. It glittered gold in the sunlight. Her fin was splashed with orange and red, almost like the beginning of a sunrise. It was beautiful, and more than she could have hoped for. "Thank you."

"Hmph," the witch grumbled. "You won't thank me when the water claims you." With a dismissive wave of her hand, the witch stepped towards the cave. Just before she reached it, the witch faded, and then vanished all together.

Cassandra shuddered then looked out to the ocean.

Nimue was waiting for her.

Chapter 5: The Curse of the Ocean

Grunting, Cassandra pushed herself into the waves. She used her arms to carry her until it grew deep enough she could slip below the surface. The water rushed through her hair and over her scales. Her hands took on webbing, like Nimue's. She grinned and started to swim.

It was a moment before she realized she was holding her breath.

Cassandra breathed in.

In an instant, her lungs felt as if they burst into flames.

The pain was so great, Cassandra cried out into the water. She rolled onto her back and clutched her chest. What had the witch done to her? Each breath brought tears of pain to her eyes.

She almost swam back to the witch and demanded her legs to be returned, but she couldn't bring herself to do it. No matter the pain, she had to find Nimue.

With lungs burning, and eyes spilling tears into the water, Cassandra swam through the ocean, searching frantically for her mermaid. Through the storms that rocked the sky, and the waves, she traveled, never once stopping.

A blinding flash of lightning finally gave her pause. She looked up at the surface and swam to the top where a great gust struck her. Cassandra was flung around like a toy until she was able to right herself. Storm clouds twisted around above her. Lightning tore through the sky and thunder rumbled.

Suddenly, a bolt crashed into the side of a ship riding the waves. The sails were set aflame, and men screamed for mercy.

Another lightning streak appeared, but instead of coming from the sky, it snarled off of the tip of a golden trident sticking out of the water. The figure holding it pointed it at the ship and sent lightning ripping through the hull. The ship cracked and groaned, the timber's bending beneath the force of the magical blows.

Cassandra dove beneath the water and traveled towards the doomed vessel. Maybe she could save someone, just as Nimue had rescued her. She swam with all the strength she had in her body and tried to ignore the burning in her chest, but it wasn't something she could just push aside.

She broke the surface again.

The ship had already started to sink. Sailors leapt into the water or crowded lifeboats. Cassandra made to go towards them when she saw the trident point towards the boats. Lightning crashed into the sailors, killing some instantly, and shattering boats so that the rest of the souls would perish in the ocean.

The figure clutched the trident tightly then turned.

Cassandra clapped a hand over her mouth in horror.

"Nimue? Nimue!" she shouted.

Nimue's eyes sparkled with tears and the same golden magic as the trident. "Cassandra!" She looked at the trident and lowered it quickly as if to hide it, but it was no use. "I-It's not what you think."

"How could you?" Cassandra cried.

Nimue opened her mouth to respond then frowned. "How are you here?"

Cassandra swam towards her, her golden tail breaking the surface momentarily.

Nimue gasped. "But...how?"

"A witch changed me," Cassandra answered then looked at the ship. "Nimue...those people. What have you done?" Even as she spoke, another man disappeared beneath the water.

Nimue clutched the trident to her chest. "You don't understand. I-I-I have to do this." She stretched out her arm and another shot of lightning shattered the final life boat.

"It was you…" Cassandra whispered. "You sank my ship!"

"I can explain!"

But Cassandra shook her head and swam backwards, horrified. All those lives…all those ships! How could Nimue do this?

She looked at the men floundering and sinking. The least she could do was save them. Cassandra dove towards them, her lungs once more setting aflame. She reached out for the men, but could only watch in despair as they sank into the ocean. The lower she went, the more her lungs burned until she had to return to the surface.

The remnants of the ship were gone, and not a single soul remained. Nimue lowered her trident. The wind stilled, the water calmed, and the dark clouds started to dissipate. She looked at Cassandra with such grief that it gave her pause. A truly evil person wouldn't look so remorseful. "I'm sorry," Nimue said and then vanished beneath the water.

"No!" Cassandra followed her. She stretched out her hand towards the mermaid, sucking in painful, salty breaths. Nimue kept a great distance between them. Cassandra faltered. She couldn't stop herself from sobbing in pain.

The sound must have carried to Nimue, because the mermaid paused. She looked back up at Cassandra.

Cassandra could see the conflict in her eyes. For a moment, she dreaded that Nimue would leave her.

Instead, Nimue swam up to her and reached out, taking Cassandra's arm in her webbed hand. "Cassandra, what is it? Are you hurt?"

"I-It hurts to breathe," Cassandra panted. She touched her throat and coughed. The clear water suddenly took on a red tint. "I had to find you, but I never thought—"

"I didn't want to do it," Nimue said. "It was the only way I could save my mother."

Cassandra frowned in confusion. "What do you mean?"

Nimue opened and shut her mouth. With a cry of frustration, she grabbed her aqua hair in her hand. "My mother fell ill, and I searched for aid. None of our healers could help her, and I just... I couldn't lose her. So I went to the one person I thought could help."

"Who? Who was it?"

Nimue covered her face. "Davy Jones."

Chapter 6: True Love's Kiss

Cassandra was stricken. Every sailor and villager knew about the monster lurking beneath the waves. He claimed the souls of fallen sailors and trapped unwary hearts in his unholy oaths. "What did you promise him?"

Nimue whimpered. "I told him I would do anything to save my mother. I signed his contract and promised a boon. He saved her, but then when he asked for the price..." She looked at the trident in her hands. "He gave me the power of a goddess. If I send him 1,000 souls, then he'll free me and my mother. If I don't, he'll kill her and force her soul into his service." Nimue shuddered. "I only attack monsters. Slavers. Murderers. But I save the innocent."

"That's why you rescued me," Cassandra realized.

"I couldn't let you die, not at my hands." Nimue laughed bitterly. "And then, I got to know you, and we grew close, and I was so afraid that you would get trapped in this oath too. I couldn't let that happen to you."

Cassandra swam closer, her chest tightening, and not just because of the ocean's curse. "Why?"

Nimue's cheeks colored. "Because, I lo—"

Whatever she meant to say was suddenly drowned out by an insidious laugh.

Nimue cried out and pushed Cassandra protectively behind her, the trident pointed forward in defense.

A figure emerged from the dark waters, two golden eyes peering out at them.

"Well," the man said. "You disappointment me, Nimue. You swore to me you killed every sailor on each ship. You dare lie to me?"

The man...the creature...sped forward and stopped inches away from Nimue's face. In the golden light, Cassandra could truly see the hideous figure of Davy

Jones.

He was a mix of human, octopus, and merman. His face bore tentacles that curled and twitched in the air. A tail that was little more than bone and several loose clumps of flesh and scales carried him through the water. But his eyes looked human, and his hands, though webbed, were powerful and huge. They fisted as if to strike Nimue.

For a moment, Cassandra saw her husband instead of Davy Jones.

She yanked Nimue back. "Don't touch her!" she snarled, only to cough and send more blood into the ocean.

"Cassandra!"

Davy Jones grinned slowly (at least she thought it was a grin). "Has my little mermaid fallen in love?" He practically spat the word. "Well, this changes things."

"N-no, please," Nimue begged. "I will continue doing your bidding. She has no part in this."

"I beg to differ," Davy Jones replied. He stared hard at Cassandra. "In fact, this may work better for you. I'll ask for a different boon. One that can free you this very moment." He pointed a sharp nail at Cassandra. "Kill one more time, and both you and your mother will go free."

"No!" Nimue sobbed. "You can't ask me to do that!"

Cassandra squared her shoulders as Davy Jones' laughter rippled around them. Each breath stabbed her in the chest, but nothing felt as painful as the monster's request. She looked back at Nimue as the mermaid sobbed and clung to the trident.

Davy Jones swam closer. "Do it, Nimue, and you can be free. Otherwise, I will take your mother now."

Cassandra glanced at him. "One more soul, that's all you require?" she asked. When he nodded, Cassandra sighed. She went to Nimue and touched her hand. "Nimue, hush. You want to save innocent lives? Then save your mother's. Save the sailors. What's one more death?"

She coughed again and touched her lips. Breathing was becoming harder, and the water was turning a deeper shade of red. "I may not be long for this world anyway."

Nimue shook her head and pulled Cassandra to her chest, dropping the trident in her haste. Cassandra caught it before it was lost. "I can't! I love you!"

Cassandra's eyes stung with unshed tears. "I love you, too," she whispered in her ear. Then she took Nimue's hand and put it over the trident. "And because I love you, I want to help you."

"Enough talk!" Davy Jones growled. He came up behind Cassandra. "Do it, or I'll fetch your mother!"

Nimue met her eyes, her face twisted with grief.

Cassandra just smiled. "Trust me," she whispered. "Take the trident."

Nimue's hand closed slowly around the golden handle. Cassandra nodded and held Nimue's hands. She turned the trident, pointing it towards stomach even as Nimue wept.

Taking a deep breath, Cassandra squeezed Nimue's hands, and trust the trident forward.

Cassandra shifted at the last second and pushed the trident up.

The trident slid past her body and stabbed directly into Davy Jones' chest.

The creature gasped in pain.

He looked down, his tentacles freezing in shock.

Cassandra glowered. "You didn't say which soul." With a grunt, she twisted the trident. "Now, Nimue!"

Nimue pulled herself from her shock and commanded the magic. Golden light filled Davy Jones' body. He managed a tortured scream before the magic disintegrated him right before their eyes. As the fragments of his body vanished, the trident crumbled.

Cassandra and Nimue watched the ocean carry the pieces away, leaving them in the calm. She flicked her tail and breathed out a sigh, but with it came a ragged cough. It shook her chest and made every nerve in her body burn with pain.

Nimue shouted her name and caught her. Cassandra's breaths came in weak wheezes. The world started to dim around her, darkness crawling in at the edges. She blinked a few times then looked up at Nimue. Weakly, she placed her hand on Nimue's soft cheek. "I'm sorry."

"Don't leave me," Nimue pleaded with her. She pulled Cassandra close. "Please, Cassandra. I can't let you go."

Cassandra forced a pained smile. "One kiss... before I go?"

Nimue bowed her head. With a soft sob, she pressed her warm limps against Cassandra's.

The world vanished for a moment, and only they two existed. Cassandra kissed her back deeply, forgetting the pain. All that mattered was Nimue.

Cassandra pulled back with a smile.

She took a breath.

There was no pain.

Nimue touched her cheek. "Cassandra?"

"I can breathe!" She laughed and spun Nimue around before kissing her back.

Nimue broke the kiss this time. "But how?"

Another voice, this one familiar, answered. "Davy Jones' hold on the ocean is gone."

Cassandra and Nimue looked up as a giant purple crab swam towards them. On his back was the witch, still covered in her fishnet dress. But this time, she bore a silvery tail. The golden trident rested in her hand.

"My spell is complete. Without Davy Jones' here, the curse on the ocean is gone. Oh, and your kiss helped a little."

Nimue frowned. "How?"

The witch winked. "True love's kiss. My spell just needed a little kick." She laughed and leaned back on the crab. "Let's leave these two beauties alone." The crab made a rumbling noise then started to swim away.

"Wait!" Cassandra cried, raising her hand. "Who are

you?"

"Oh, I go by many names," the witch said over her shoulder. "But you can just call me Calypso." With another laugh, both the witch and the crab vanished.

Cassandra shook her head and looked at Nimue. The mermaid beamed at her and pulled her to her chest. Cassandra buried her head into her mermaid's beautiful hair.

In that moment, she knew that she had finally found real love.

Two-Sentence Horror Stories

Various Authors

The following is the result of a particularly popular writing exercise at the Cedar Room, wherein writers were asked to write a complete horror story in the space of two sentences.

He smiled down at me, warming my already overflowing heart, as he lifted me over the threshold, flower petals still clinging to the shoulder of his tailored tux. As the door shut behind him, he said, "Now that we're married, I have a confession," as his warm brown eyes bled into all white, like smooth enameled china.

— Leslie Kung

The low, steady rain soaked into the earth. There was a faint smell of bitter almonds.

— Alexandra Penn

I tapped my fingers against the armrest as I waited for the flight attendant to finish up her conversation with the woman in white so I could ask for a blanket. I didn't know that the sudden temperature drop was connected to the woman until she dug her fingers into either side of the flight attendant's face and sucked all the warmth and life out of her in an instant.

— Leslie Kung

Low in the sky above a calm sea, the moon rose each night. Each night, it came a little closer.

— Alexandra Penn

The children played happily on the playground equipment. They laughed, clapped and opened their mouths to the sky when it began to rain blood.

— Leslie Kung

For years, Maizy cried whenever I put her to bed. That all stopped when my hand decomposed.

— Erin Casey

A bustling city boasted a population of 600,000 people. Then it didn't.

— Alexandra Penn

Ticket sales dropped dramatically after the star was filmed fat shaming her musical co-star. When she left the stage and dropped off the radar without warning, everyone assumed it was the diva's response to being blacklisted, not because she'd been dragged below stage after hours by disjointed mannequins and long snaking tendrils of wigs.

— Leslie Kung

The ball bounced three times in the empty hallway and came to a stop.

It came to a stop two feet off the ground.

— Leslie Kung

The deer bedded down for the night, stamping the grass down beneath their hooves and surrounding the young with the protection of the old. In the morning, they continued down the freeway unharmed.

— Alexandra Penn

Carol felt a cool kiss on the back of her neck and breathed in her husband's musky cologne. She'd put him in a grave five years ago.

— Erin Casey

There was a breath of air and a kiss of sunlight before the door closed. He did not repeat the experience for some time.

— Alexandra Penn

"Turn off your phone alarm, Janice," Greg mumbled as he pushed his face further into his pillow. Then his eyes shot open as he remembered that Janice had died last year in the fire, and he'd picked up the half-melted iPhone off what used to be the dining room floor as he wept.

— Leslie Kung

At bedtime, his mother sang him to sleep in a quiet soprano. At breakfast, she greeted him signing.

— Alexandra Penn

"BoooOOOOoooOOO!" said the ghost, waving its arms and bobbing in the air. The glassy-eyed child did not respond.

— Alexandra Penn

Nikki Herbst

Nikki Herbst is a lifelong writer who came to Iowa City many years ago to attend the Iowa Writers' Workshop and liked the community so much that she moved here a few years later. She has a novel that she's "finished" many times and another one that she's started many times. Her poems have appeared in Denver Quarterly, The Antioch Review, The North American Review, The Georgia Review, Black Warrior Review, and a dozen other journals. She's very happy to be a co-concierge, with Maxwell Love, of The Golden Attic, where poetry fun and magic will be ongoing. She invites everyone to visit her poetry/photography site, www.flyingtrapeze.net, or to find her on Facebook, where they will see posts about her work with birds of prey, her travels around the country to teach folk dance, and other passions.

The Beggar Boy

Nikki Herbst

I am the first
the last
the only
I am but one of a thousand million
I have all the food in the world
in a bombed-out larder
all of the muscles a hard life can gift
every angle corner curve and slope of this city
to hurry along
hide behind
forget to remember
and coins
I have coins
of apple-flesh oak callous eggshell
coins in every pocket and at every bend of my body
like old men grasping each other's knuckles in a game
    of cunning
I have a warm bed of grit green glass shards thistle
a nest lined with lost shanks of hair from nameless
    women
a blanket of matted leaves cooked dry by day
Every dwelling is mine from sewer to roof
a mountain range of half walls shattered floorboards
windows released to a million knives
no privilege of stairs no prison of
I have time
I have no time
Time has no me
Water is not
like a gift of lying still by choice
It spills through the holes in my heart vision hands
I have all the cloth I need

to carry nothing hide nothing warm nothing bind
        nothing
I have a language of words and silence
pauses gushes the high-pitched buzzing of wheatears
All that I say is true
in a false place with no sentences
I say 'please' because you must
I say 'you' because you are
Love me. Love me. Love me.

All The Children At Bedtime

Nikki Herbst

An hour before sunset they start
up from the cornfields
in twos, in threes, in groups of eight or ten
or a hundred, all over the land they kettle up,
riding the thermals, crying out. Our children
rise and circle, circle and rise, pump their
plump arms and glide toward the river.
Wave after wave of them,
hundreds, then thousands, then
hundreds of thousands,
splaying their dirt-caked toes, legs outstretched
as they settle on the water,
calling for their mamas.
Some are splashed clean without protest.
Some want a lullaby, the light from the sun
    left on,
a drink, a story,
just one more song, please, just one.
No one forgets to come home. No one is kept
from coming home. No one stays in the
    cornfields.
Islands of young, islands of well-fed, sleepy
children stowed for the night, dreaming
of corn and each other. They came home
again. They came home again.
They'll rise before dawn and fly back to the corn
and come home again.

They'll do this forever.
They've done this forever. Our round children.
Our flying, calling children.

What It's Like To Be Adopted

Nikki Herbst

Ah, my pretties, there was a *stillness*—
think of it as sphere-shaped
a ping-pong ball without the ball—
and perhaps before that grand explosions
around other emptinesses. Our stillness
collapsed, smashed itself white and blue
flew red and purple
out, we say. Flew to what
we call *here* and *there*.

Sweet ones, the pieces moved this far and
that far until
divided by *now* and *then* we called their changes
speed, their journeys *time*.
We call our game *knowledge*
as we hold hands and live its fun and terror
for, dearest listeners, each particle attracts all
    others
so we know of *gravity*, *love*, *luminosity*,
and the shifts of momentum called *history*.

We play here
in this tiny history
the balls we toss falling
(where we call *down*) like the bits
of what we do not know
flying toward the center of another

stillness
before they what we call *begin*
what we call *again.*

Urtext

Nikki Herbst

> *In addition to meaning the skin of an*
> *animal and the act of concealing, the word*
> *'hide' used to refer to the amount of land*
> *needed for one free family and its dependents.*

The Good Girl sleeps quietly
with other women's husbands.
Dimples cast in concrete,
she cleaves a breast of white meat;
a potato bursts in the oven.

At first, the word 'win' meant merely to struggle.

Homeostasis: maintaining a couch,
a fire, a coffee table behind your ribs,
fine art on your turbulent heart.

At first, 'attack' meant to stick a tack into.

The Good Girl has forgiven music
for the pain it has caused her.
Bathing herself in vanilla and almonds,
she gets a job and keeps it,
collecting her pay like rainwater
in clean pools and pockets.

Here are the morning, the noon, and the night,
her silent partners, investors
in waiting, their solar and lunar coins
strung out like a dazzling bracelet
shimmering a dance of lust.

ALSO CHECK OUT
THE WRITERS' ROOMS

Local to the Iowa area? Interested in writing?

The Writers' Rooms seeks to tap into the wealth of information shared by local writers. Our writing community has the amazing benefit of a massive collection of backgrounds, experiences, and viewpoints. The Writers' Rooms endeavors to bring these wonderful ideas together and help all writers with their craft. We strive to encourage and foster community-based knowledge to help lead literary sessions and provide a safe, positive writing environment.

Our Rooms are moderated by both our Concierges and the members of our community. Community-led sessions tap into the wealth of our collective knowledge, allowing our writers to both share their own experiences and learn from other attendees.

Find out more at www.TheWritersRooms.org!

You can also like our page on Facebook (IAWritersRooms), and follow us on Instagram (@WritersRooms) and Twitter (@IAWritersRooms).

THE COMMUNITY
ANTHOLOGIES

The Writers' Rooms strives to provide opportunities to our communities: therefore, along with the Concierge Anthologies, we have open submissions once a year for Community Anthologies as well! These anthologies are all-genre books that put our writers front and center.

Each year, a theme is announced at the beginning of an open call for submissions. Our first Community Anthology, *Writers of the Depths*, will focus on the theme "underwater", and will be released in 2019.

Learn more at www.TheWritersRooms.org!